Cast The
CARDS

BY
SHYLA COLT

DEDICATIONS

To my family, friends, and fans who've joined me on this wild ride!

Chapter One

Cool night air caressed bare arms, and Savannah shivered. Questioning her outfit of choice, she stepped closer to Clark. The sleeveless, plum-colored dress with the gold, Egyptian pattern, empire waist, and flaring skirt had been fierce in the heat of the day. But with the sun gone down it was freezing.

"Cold?" Clark asked in his soothing baritone.

"A little."

"Here." He shrugged out of his lightweight, brown leather jacket and helped her slide her arms inside the too-long sleeves. His chivalry melted her like chocolate candy in the sun. If she wasn't already head over strappy-heeled sandals for him, she'd be falling.

Now I just need to tell him. When her childhood best friend Clark and his identical twin Carey had opted to attend the community college for their first two years alongside her, she'd been ecstatic. They'd been the Three Musketeers since diapers. Separating would have ripped her heart out before she jumped into the biggest adventure of her life. Freshman year felt like a continuance of high school. Yet, somewhere between the start of sophomore year and now things had shifted.

She saw Clark in a brand new light. When he'd asked her to go to the carnival and Carey had bowed out, she saw the opportunity she'd been waiting for.

His scent permeated the jacket, and she pulled it closer, inhaling. *Sandalwood and worn leather.*

"Such a gentleman."

"'Course, Vannah. Couldn't let you freeze to death. Our parents would kill me." They took a step forward as the group ahead of them entered the funhouse.

"So what's after this?" she asked.

"Tunnel of Love and then head back to the dorms?" He inclined his head toward her.

"Sounds good." *If you still want to talk to me after what I plan on pulling in the tunnel.*

"You okay? You seem far away." He cocked an eyebrow, dipping his head to meet her gaze. His hair fell across his forehead and into his eyes. Concern darkened his blue-green eyes to a beautiful turquoise. She longed to push the silken strands back and tuck it behind the ears that curved slightly at the tips.

He brushed the locks back impatiently, breaking the spell he'd held her under.

"Yeah, just hoping there are no clowns inside."

"Still afraid of clowns?" He smirked.

"Yes, they're creepy. It should never be socially accepted to hide your true identity under make-up, and constantly perform odd rituals."

"Rituals?" His lips twitched with repressed laughter.

"Yes, seltzer bottles of water, pies in the face. It's like clowns have a chloroform rag at the ready, waiting for the moment you let your guard down and turn your back." Crossing her arms under her chest, she huffed.

"I think you've been reading too much Stephen King." He shook his head.

"Mock me all you want. If we get into that place and a clown comes after me I'm screaming that bitch down."

He laughed, shaking his head. "I could just see that too." His

2

gaze focused on something behind her. "Looks like we'll find out soon. It's our turn."

Her heart smacked against her ribs, and her stomach plummeted into her shoes. She didn't feel right. Everything in her screamed "go back". Clark moved forward and she hesitated.

"Vannah?" He frowned, concern etched all over his face.

I can't wuss out. He loves fun houses.

"I'm ready." She gave a shaky smile, forced one foot in front of the other, and followed him up the stairs.

"Step right in to the house of a million faces," said the ride worker in black jeans and a black t-shirt. Clark wrapped an arm around Savannah's waist and squeezed.

At least something good is coming out of this. Smoke obscured her vision as they walked inside a dimly-lit hallway. A jack-in-the-box sprung out near the end, and she screamed.

"Wound tight, are we?" Amusement colored Clark's voice.

"Shut up."

They continued into a large room with multiple mirrors surrounding them.

"Which way?" he asked.

"Left?"

"You got it."

They turned and found themselves at a dead end. A strange sense of urgency hit her.

"Let's hurry up and find our way out of here, please." She tugged him to the right. The hair on the back of her neck stood on end, her skin prickled with fear. As they found the proper passage she glanced over her shoulder to see a stern-faced clown with dead eyes. His garish white face was highlighted with bright red lips and red and blue circles around the eyes. Bright orange hair stuck out from underneath a dingy red hat.

Vannah's breath caught in her throat, and she urged Clark to go faster, almost stumbling in her haste to get away.

"Whoa. Calm down." Normally his voice soothed but tonight the effect was lost on her.

"Clown. I saw a clown." They passed through a glow-in-the dark room and out into the night. Once they cleared the doorframe her psyche sang with joy. Bending over, she gulped down air as he rubbed her back.

"Hey, we can head home now if you want."

Yes! "No, I'd like to go to the Tunnel if you don't mind. It's always been my favorite ride."

"It would be."

She peered up at him and smiled. The light from the carnival rides sliced through the night and highlighted his beautiful face. With a father from Spain and a blonde mother with green eyes, he was born to be gorgeous. He had a thin, muscular frame covered in olive-colored skin, a strong jaw, and chocolate brown hair that fell into his beautiful eyes just so.

"What's wrong with being a romantic?" She elbowed him in the side.

"Nothing if you're an English major." The amusement in his tone softened his words.

"Whatever, Mr. Undeclared." She straightened up to her full five feet eleven inches. "Let's head over to the Tunnel."

They walked the thirty feet in comfortable silence. The Tunnel looked deserted. Giant swan-shaped boats were lined up with no other carnival goers or ride operators in sight. There was something ominous in the stillness.

"Looks like you're the only one who likes this thing," he said.

"Yeah." She scanned the area. "Maybe it's closed? We can just leave."

As soon as the words left her lips a man appeared in a Vaudeville outfit. A straw hat set on top of his head. The red-and-white pinstriped sports jacket, white button-up, red bowtie, and white pants were straight out of the nineteen fifties.

"Step right up to the Tunnel of Love, folks." It should have been charming. Instead, it made her skin crawl. She tugged her borrowed jacket closer to ward off the coldness that threatened to seep into her bones. Clark ushered her over to the boat, holding her hand as she stepped down into the vehicle that bobbed in the water.

"Enjoy your ride." There was a strange look in the operator's eyes she couldn't quite place. Watching him over her shoulder as the Swan began to drift into the darkened passageway, a frown turned down the corners of her lips.

"Did he seem strange to you?" She turned her gaze to Clark.

"We are at a carnival."

"Yeah, that's true." She smiled.

Ducking down to eye level, he stared. "Are you sure you're okay?"

"There was actually something I wanted to tell you." She toyed with the ring on her finger, spun it around to disperse negative energy as she trained her gaze on her lap.

"What's up? You know you can tell me anything. That's what best friends are for." Their boat bumped the one in front of them. "Pile up in the Tunnel of Love."

She laughed, but her heart wasn't in it. The apprehension from earlier returned.

"What were you going to say?" he redirected the conversation.

"That." She glanced up at him and froze when she caught a glimpse of a shape in the darkness. The clown from earlier was right behind him. Her throat seemed to swell and her tongue felt thick and clumsy as she opened her mouth to warn him.

"Cl—"

A cloth covered her mouth. Her scream ended before it began. The sweet, chemical smell assaulted her senses, and she knew no more.

Her eyes fluttered open and she was met with an intense darkness. She swallowed in an attempt to moisten the Sahara

Desert of her mouth. Her head pounded. A humming filled her ear, and the gentle rocking motion told her it was a vehicle of some sort. She tried to move her limbs and couldn't.

They'd bound her.

Panic set in. She rolled, made contact with something solid, and returned to her former position. Her head spun and her stomach churned. A grunt spilled into the air.

"Clark?" Her voice was scratchy. The whispered word was painful.

"Yeah. I'm here." He sounded weak.

She did her best to look in the direction his voice had come from but ropes restrained her. "Are you okay?"

"I think so… What happened?"

"We-we've been kidnapped." She wiggled her wrists, trying to loosen the rope. "We have to get out of here. There's no way they plan on letting us go. Neither of us comes from a wealthy family, so it can't be a ransom situation." A heartbeat passed. "Clark?"

"We can get out of here. My dad's helped design cars for years. Somewhere in here there should be a release latch. Look over my shoulder. Do you see anything giving off light?"

She focused on his words, scanned the area, and caught a tiny spot with a green hue. "Yes."

"Good, scoot over here. I don't want them to hear us. What you're seeing should be the trunk release mechanism. It can be a lever, handle, or cord."

"I want you to direct me to it." She fought to keep her rapid breathing under control, but the darkness was suffocating. *Steady, won't be any good to him passed out.* Shock had begun to wear and in its place, terror had taken a foothold.

"Okay." Her voice shook, but she held it together by the grace of God and the will to survive that got people through when all they wanted to do was break down. Since the area was impossible to see, she guess-timated where his body lay. "Scoot back." She heard the whisper of cloth. "I think you need to scoot up." More rustling then a thud.

"Ow. This is as far as I can go." He wiggled, blocked the glow. "Okay… I got it. Next time this car stops or slows we're getting out. Come as close to me as you can get."

She rolled over to him, pressed her body to his. Time passed. Minutes, hours, there was no way to tell really. The driver applied the brakes.

"Ready?" Clark asked.

"Yes." She nodded.

The car came to a complete stop. A click sounded. *He pulled the handle. Be ready.* Her muscles tensed. The trunk popped. She sat up, pushed it open with her body, and found herself tumbling. He'd shoved her forward and out the car with the momentum of his body. The ground rushed up to meet her and she curled into a ball, rolling to the side.

She landed onto a hard surface. Her body took the brunt of the fall but the side of her face struck. The world spun. Beating back the dizziness, she struggled to assimilate. The squeal of tires mingled with the sound of yelling and feet pounding over pavement. The smell of burned rubber seared her nostrils.

Her vision wavered and came back in focus. An older gentleman with white hair and kind brown eyes kneeled in front of her.

"Miss, are you all right?"

"Clark, where's Clark?"

"There was someone else in there with you?"

"Oh God."

"We're calling the police now, ma'am. Help's on the way."

Leaning over, she vomited. Tears streamed down her face. She knew with a certainty that broke the foundation of her world in two that she'd never see Clark Carr again, and it was all her fault.

⊰⊱

PRESENT DAY

Carey woke with a sick feeling in his stomach. It was the anniversary of the day Clark disappeared. He always got drunk the night before. *The one time I opt out of doing something with my twin and everything goes to shit. I can't help but wonder if having three people there would've deterred the kidnappers. Not that I'll ever know.*

He usually avoided torturing himself with what-ifs but today was its own special brand of hell. His thoughts drifted to Savannah and a sudden urge for a hair from the dog that bit him hit. A shot of Jack wouldn't hurt anyone. Who cared that it was—he glanced at the alarm clock beside his bed—seven in the morning? The pain wouldn't have been so bad had it been shared. Unfortunately, his pseudo sister could barely look him in the eye. She felt so guilty about it. Henceforth the permanent split of what had once been the Three Musketeers.

It had been like losing two parts of himself instead of one. She was a big shot F.B.I. agent now over at Quantico, but she'd be at the grave this year, same as always. It was the one time a year he knew he'd see her, though they never talked, just stood at the grave, sometimes not even together. She looked good on the outside, tall, lithe, and put together. Still, he guessed she never really healed, because he didn't hear about her having any male suitors, or female for that matter.

She lived for her job profiling. *Pot meet Kettle.* It wasn't as if he had much going on outside of his gig as a cop. *Never thought the name Carey Carr would be synonymous with Protect and Serve— I was usually the one raising the hell.* He sat up with a groan, forced his weary body from the bed, and stumbled to the bathroom. When he walked through the door he did a double-take. Clark stood by the shower stall in the exact same outfit he'd last seen him in—brown boots, jeans, white undershirt, brown, blue and white-plaid button up and a brown leather jacket.

8

"Damn … I might have to leave whiskey alone if it's going to make me hallucinate."

"I'm not a hallucination, Carey."

"Isn't that what they all say?" He shook his head. "This shit it too fricking weird for me. Turn your head, Imaginary Clark. I gotta drain the lizard."

"Why? It looks exactly the same as what I have."

"Nice to know even in my head you're still a smartass." Carey shook his head, freed his dick from his boxer briefs, and aimed into the toilet.

"Aren't you going to ask me why I'm here?" Imaginary Clark asked.

"Pretty obvious. Half a bottle of whiskey mixed with guilt and some anniversary angst."

"Why haven't I shown up before?"

"I don't know? Can you ask me this when my head doesn't feel like it's being ripped apart by a jackhammer?"

Clark sighed. "Come on, Carey, you're better than this."

"Hey! You don't get to come in here on your ghost cloud and judge me. Life without you is the hardest shit I've ever done, especially since Van split. Fuck I'm talking to myself!" He snorted.

"You're really not."

This time Carey ignored Clark, flushed, moved to the shower, and turned the spray on as hot as he could stand it. He pulled down his boxers, kicked them toward the hamper, and stepped inside the basin. With his head under the water he clenched his eyes tight and prayed to God when he left the stall *Ghost Clark* would be gone.

I know I don't talk to you like I should, but please take this away. I can't. Ten minutes and a good scrub-down later, Carey felt like a new man. The hangover was tolerable, and the smell of alcohol had run down the drain. It was time to get something in his stomach. He stepped out of the shower and sighed. No Clark. Toweling dry, he padded into his room, slipped on a pair of comfy black sweats, a plain black T-shirt, and migrated to the kitchen. He opened the refrigerator and jumped when Clark appeared to his right.

"I'm sorry, I really hate to do this to you, but it's important."

"Damnit!"

"Please, believe it's me. You want me to Swayze something?" The refrigerator door jerked out of his hand and closed.

Carey's hand shook. Afraid to believe, he hesitated. "Clark?"

"Yes. I'm really here, and you need to pay attention because this is about Savannah."

Carey took a shaky breath and nodded. "Okay, this is happening."

"You believe me now?" Clark leaned closer.

"That or I'm completely insane which isn't likely to just happen overnight." He clung to the logic in his response. When all logical answers failed it was time to think outside the box. Extending a shaky hand, he touched Clark's arm and jumped.

"You're solid!"

"Jeez. Nice to see your own deductive reasoning outweighs my mad ghost skills."

Carey smirked. "I don't want to get sappy, but I've missed you, asshole." His voice broke and he cleared his throat to dislodge the lump that choked him. He threw an arm around his brother, hugging his body to him as tears escaped his eyes. Clark's body was whole, albeit cooler than normal, as he returned the hug.

"I would've come sooner if I could've, I swear. It doesn't work that way."

"I'm just glad you're here now." Pulling back, Carey wiped his eyes with the back of his hand. Clark's words from earlier registered, bursting his bubble of joy. "You said this was about Vannah?"

"Yes, she's in danger."

"Hate to break it to you, little brother, but that's kind of in her job description."

10

"Younger by one minute, ass, and not this kind of danger… They're back." The whispered tone was full of apprehension. *Why would a ghost be scared?*

"Who?"

"The killers who took us want to finish what they started."

"Over my dead fucking body." Carey balled his hand into a fist.

"That's what I was hoping you said," Clark whispered, a look of relief on his face.

"Tell me what I need to do."

"First, speak to her."

"Easier said than done, Clark." He ran a hand through his hair and blew out air.

"What happened between you two?"

"I don't know. Things got fucked up quick. Maybe seeing your face when she looked at me was too much? She pulled away, went inside her own head, and never really came back out. Next thing I know she's switching schools, her major, and avoiding me like the plague. I tried to contact her for a while, and then I just…" Carey shrugged. "I figured if she needed me to back off to be okay, then that's what I'd do. It hurt like a bitch though. I won't lie."

"That doesn't sound like her." Clark looked crestfallen.

Carey's heart bled for him. *Poor guy comes back and everything is upside down.*

"That carefree girl who wanted to teach impressionable young minds and heal the world one person at a time is long gone, Clark. I'm sorry."

Clark ducked his head and nodded. "No, I knew she wouldn't be the same. I just hoped…"

"I know. " Carey sniffed, sucked back tears. *Time for a safer topic.* "You said the people that did this to you are back?"

"Yes, they've been at this game a long time. There have been more victims than anyone can imagine."

"Why? What's their motive?" The senseless violence people

inflicted on others sickened and confused him. You have an issue so you take it out on an innocent victim?

"I don't know. I'm not told everything. I do know you need to stay close to Savannah. It's a matter of life or death. She needs someone to watch her back at all times, and you're the only one I trust to do that."

"I hate to break it to you but she runs with the big dogs. The F.B.I . I'm a lowly police sergeant in Dale."

"It's not going to matter." Clark shook his head. "They'll bring this fight to your doorstep."

"What do you mean?" Goosebumps broke out over Carey. Silence stretched between them. "Clark?"

Clark's demeanor changed. The spark left his eyes and his shoulders slumped. "You'll see. I have to go now."

"Are you kidding me? Right now?"

"Get in touch with Vannah. It's important." Clark's form wavered.

"Don't you leave me with that half-cocked answer!"

"This isn't on my terms –" Clark disappeared in mid-sentence.

"Fuck!" Turning, he slammed his fist into the wall. Pain radiated up his fingers. He hugged the injured hand to his chest.

Did that really just happen? If I was smart I'd cook myself breakfast and forget the whole thing. The idea sounded good. If there was as remote chance Clark had been here, he'd do what he asked. Despite everything, he still cared about Savannah, and he'd do anything for his brother.

Looks like I'm in for a trip down memory lane. Whether Savannah wants it or not.

Chapter Two

W^{est."}

Savannah looked up from her desk and frowned. It never failed—the second she was trying to leave the office something important needed tending. "What's up, Davis?"

"Package for you." The dark-haired man held up a manila envelope and shook it back and forth.

"Thanks." She took the yellow square from him and placed it in her weekend satchel. She always took a few days off this time of year.

"When you headed back this way?" Davis's brow furrowed as she locked her desk, zipped up her satchel, and stood.

"What? You gonna miss me?" She lifted an eyebrow and smirked.

Davis rolled his eyes. "You wish, West."

They'd butted heads when he first joined the team, but now they had a sibling-like relationship. Their quips were in jest.

"I'll be here Monday, bright and early, ready to whip you back into shape." Winking, she turned to her partner. "I'll see you Monday, Blanton."

"I'll hold down the fort while you're gone."

She snorted. "Right, 'cause it's a regular C.S.I. down here."

Chuckling to herself, she walked down the aisle and out of the office. If only TV viewers knew how dull profiling really was.

The majority of her time was spent at a desk, hunting through papers and databases. In many ways they were almost contractors, working on whatever needed their attention at the moment. To her it was all relative. Even one step closer to catching the people who'd committed these heinous crimes was better than nothing. It was her mantra. The one thing she believed with her entire soul that kept her from going crazy.

This job could get to you if you weren't cautious. Spending so much time up to your neck in the worst-case scenarios caused erosion on your soul and mind. It was why she never got too serious with anyone. They wouldn't understand, and she didn't want the vulnerability that came along with love.

Her mind turned to the event that had shattered her life. Most people were fortunate enough to live under the assumption they were safe from the horrible tragedies that happened in the news. She'd learned at twenty-one that was bullshit.

Quantico was close enough to her hometown to get back within a couple of hours—the perfect amount of miles to keep her distance while remaining involved. She loved her parents, but they expected her to return to the person she'd once been, before Clark's death. She never could.

It was painful having to choose between whom she needed to be and who they wanted her to be. Marriage and kids weren't even a blip on her radar. There was too much to do. How could she ever be truly happy when Clark's murderers were still on the loose, he was in the ground, and the world seemed to go to hell a little more each day?

When she reached her black SUV she placed her satchel in the passenger seat, slipped behind the wheel, and started the car. She connected her MP3 player and pulled up the playlist simply titled Clark. "Lost Prophets" came through the speakers and she was taken back to that golden time when the Three Musketeers were untouched and happy.

As the music lulled her into a full-blown case of nostalgia, a fresh wave of regret and guilt broke over her. She did Carey dirty, abandoned him when he needed her most. The cowardly act haunted her. *Ironic I can hunt down hardened criminals but can't apologize to my childhood friend and move on.*

AC/DC exploded over the speakers and she laughed. This would forever remind her of the Carr boys. They inherited their father's love for classic rock and by proxy passed it on to her. She couldn't listen to anything pre-1980 without thinking of them.

As the tires ate up the road, her happy reminiscing turned somber. The question she never found an answer for her snaked its way to the forefront. *Why did I survive when Clark didn't?*

Despite how bad it made her feel, she couldn't stop picking apart her life. Had she done enough with the extra time she'd been given? Clark gave his life for hers. Did she prove her worth? By the time she pulled into the city limits she was a frazzled mess. Her hands trembled and her stomach churned like the water in the sound.

Parked outside the local florist, she stepped from the car, her wraparound black sunglasses still in place. The last thing she wanted the people to be flapping their gums about was poor Savannah West and her puffy, red eyes.

The scent of freshly-cut flowers and the cheery atmosphere were lost to her as she scanned the area from behind the safety of her lenses. A large, bright bouquet caught her gaze from inside the refrigerated case on the far right. The mix of yellows, reds, and oranges called to her like a homing beacon.

She opened the case, removed the bundle, and turned on her heel. Chill bumps broke out over her skin. Déjà vu hit. This extra sensory perception had occurred that night she'd been kidnapped. Her internal compass had become the catalyst that led her to her position in the F.B.I. Training kicked in. She did a sweep of the area from her peripheral, careful to maintain a regular gait and lax body language. When she came up empty, she chalked the unease up to the anniversary.

I hate being off my game. After the dust from the explosion of life as she knew it settled, she put Savannah West back together, piece by piece, and decided to dedicate her life to helping victims of crimes and their families. The work was hard and climbing the ladder was a nasty, no-holds-barred fight among the ranks.

Still, she had an affinity for reading people, getting into their psyche and under their skin. It was a gift she'd previously taken for granted. The nagging feeling in the back of her head that told her when a situation or a person was safe or not, the one her mother called her inner voice, served her well. Coached to listen to her inner voice from the time she was young, she never imagined it would come in handy. If only she'd listened that night.

Disgusted by the cycle she allowed to happen each year, she kept her face a blank canvas when she reached the register.

"Will that be all for you, dear?" the older woman with salt-and-pepper hair that curled around her ears asked.

"Yes, ma'am." She was a Dale transplant. It gave her the anonymity she craved.

"That's going to be $54.30."

Savannah handed over her card, lost again in the recesses of her mind. She signed the receipt, took the flowers, and walked back to her car on autopilot.

The day was gorgeous. She scowled as she parked her car on the gravel road. It should at least be overcast. Summer in Dale had always felt wrong after Clark was taken. It was a big part of why she'd switched colleges. The town that had once been her cornerstone became stifling and oppressive. The looks, whispers, and accusing stares from those who blamed her for the tragedy had become too much.

She pried her fingers from the steering wheel, grabbed the flowers from the passenger seat, and opened her door.

Then she made the walk she could probably do in her sleep. The sun beat down on her black sports coat, spreading heat across her shoulders and onto her back. The black pants, practical for work, were sweat-soaked and stuck to her upper thighs.

There was a time when she used to get dressed up for this. Now it was too damn maudlin. She rounded the last curve and paused fifty yards away. The gravesite was well-tended, the dark gray slab that bore Clark's likeness waited patiently, like an old friend. *I halfway think you're here with me, Clark.* It was why she continued to come. For these brief moments every year she stood in his presence.

Her pulse raced. The air filled with anticipation. On the cusp of an intangible event, she moved forward. In front of the grave she almost expected him to appear, the sexy smirk that made her forgive all on his lips. A strangled laugh escaped from her clogged throat.

"Only you could get me out here talking to the wind."

"Seems to me you used to do that sort of thing all the time." The deep voice made her want to cover her ears. Pain splintered her heart and water rushed to her eyes.

No. Frozen in place she held her position. There hadn't been anyone around for miles. She spun, her heart in her throat. A moment of disappointment preceded the anger. It was Carey. The years had been kind. His shoulders were broad, and his muscles appeared sinewy in the khaki pants he'd paired with a dark blue polo. The hair that used to fall into his eyes had been tamed into a spiky style reminiscent of a faux hawk. Tattoos covered his forearms. It shocked her system. In her mind's eye he'd still been that lanky boy she'd grown up with.

How could I not have heard him approach? That's not like me.

Silence stretched between them like a shaky rope ladder that needed to be traveled upon with care. She licked her lips. It was her mistake to make right. *Time to man up.*

"I owe you an apology."

17

"Really?" He mocked her with widened eyes that blazed with anger and beautiful lips that curved into a snarky expression. It hurt to look at him. She wanted to avert her gaze but he deserved better.

"Yeah. What I did was shitty, and I apologize." Shoving her hands into her pockets, she kicked at the grass.

"The great Savannah West apologizing? Should I break out my camera phone? I hear that doesn't happen too often these days."

"Are we really going to hold my job against me?"

"Not your job—the way you've become."

"What would you know about it? You think rumors circulating around the bureau mean shit to me? Come on, I'm a woman in a man's world. Of course they all think I'm a cold bitch because I don't spread my legs, or kiss and tell." Venom filled her words like poison.

"You let this job change you."

"Bullshit. This," She gestured toward the headstone with her head," did that long before any job in law enforcement."

"So you admit it then!"

"I never denied it, Carey! Why are you arguing with me? I was trying to apologize." Yanking her hands from her pockets, she threw them into the air. Infuriated by the antagonistic behavior he exhibited.

"Because it never should've taken you this long." The truth cooled her anger like a fire extinguisher to a blaze.

"Don't you think I know that?" A loud crack rent the air. She jumped. Her body tensed. She waited for the sound to come again. "Did you hear that?" she whispered.

"Yeah."

"You don't seem worried. It's not cloudy and I didn't see anyone around the perimeter." Body stiff, her gaze darted around, seeking out spots where a person could hide.

"You can't even turn it off, can you?" The disgust and sorrow in his words stung.

"We both know just because a town is small doesn't mean bad things can't happen."

"Touché, Ms. West."

She growled. "This isn't how I wanted this to go."

"I bet," he mumbled.

"I know I've been a coward when it comes to you. It's not something I'm proud of, but after a time it was just easier to keep moving forward without looking back. Back then every time I saw you it was like someone ripping open a fresh wound. It wouldn't have been good for either of us for me to hang around." She beseeched him to understand with wild hand gestures and a direct stare.

"Why couldn't you just say that?" He shook his head.

"I don't know. You're asking me for rational when I was anything but that for a long time." A sigh passed her lips.

"I can understand that. It's why I respected the distance you seemed to want to keep."

"Why break it now?"

"Because I asked him to." A cold breeze encircled her. She wrapped her arms around her waist and turned her head to the right. A face she knew as well as her own buckled her knees. Her body hit the hard ground with a loud thud. She grimaced, gritted her teeth, and blinked. No amount of eyelid flutter rid her of the apparition, if he could be called that. He seemed whole.

"C-Carey?" Her mouth wobbled, refusing to cooperate.

"Yes, I see him too."

"How? Why?" She shook her head, shoved her fist into her trembling lips to keep from blubbering like a newborn babe.

"You're in danger, Vannah. I had to come back." Clark took a step closer.

She held out her hand, shaking her head like a child throwing a temper tantrum.

"No. This isn't possible." Hyperventilating, she sank her fingers into the ground, gripping the blades of grass in her fists to stay grounded. "You hate me so much you'd stage this?" Her voice cracked, and she rocked back and forth.

"Darling, David Copperfield himself couldn't stage this," Carey said.

"I'm real, Vannah." Clark walked over and kneeled in front of her. "You have to believe me." His gaze penetrated as he peered into her soul, the same way he always had. He reached out and caressed her face with the backs of his knuckles. His touch was slightly below normal temperature, but real. She could feel the pressure exerted against her skin. Her chest tightened.

"Oh God. It's really you."

"Yes." He nodded. "I hate to rush this along, but you both need to leave here now." The urgency in his tone was a metaphorical slap that cut through her shock.

"Danger?" *Was this why he came back?*

"Fill her in, Carey. There are things happening." Clark frowned. "I have to go."

She pushed off from the ground, gained her balance, and stood to her full height. The word "danger" had triggered her training. There was no time for fear or shock.

Clark disappeared before her eyes and her jaw dropped. *I knew he was a ghost, but… Jesus.* She rotated her body and stared at Carey, barely able to contain her fury. He'd set this up. She was sure of it.

"What the fuck is going on?"

"Come on, let's go get a drink."

"You must be out of your mind if you think I'm just going to walk off with you like that didn't just happen to go have drinks as if we're BFF's out for lunch." She balled her fists, digging her fingernails into her skin as she tried to rein in her anger. The nonchalance he displayed had her spoiling for a fight.

"It's about your kidnappers."

The world shifted on its axis, knocking her on her ass mentally. Clamping her jaw shut, she closed her eyes and struggled against the mass of emotions threatening to drown her in their depths. Opening her eyes again, she nodded.

"How about we go grab that drink?" *More like an entire bottle.*

Clark watched Vannah and Carey talk. It was strange observing them like this now that he'd made initial contact. But they needed to come to an understanding on their own.

"You've made contact. How do you feel?"

He turned to the olive-skinned woman with dark hair who'd been assigned as his case worker. A guide, for lack of a better description, Zenia escorted souls here and there. She was the bridge that'd allowed him to travel from Heaven back to Earth.

"Like shit."

"Why? I thought we both agreed this was the best way to deal with your unusual attachments." She frowned. He dark eyes silently dissected him. He felt like a frog pinned to a table.

"I turned their world upside down. Returning just reminds me of how much it's no longer my world. Everything has changed, including Carey and Vannah." A wistful longing for the sweet girl who wanted to be a teacher and wore free-flowing gowns struck him.

"You knew your death affected them both greatly." Her voice was cold and distant. The robotic response jarred his ears like nails on a chalkboard. She'd been otherworldly for so long she'd forgotten what being human truly felt like. But he never had. That was the problem. It was impossible to enjoy Heaven when your heart and your mind were stuck on the day-to day. He'd spent an unhealthy amount of time viewing their lives like a movie played on a big screen.

"Yes, but seeing it from a distance and experiencing it for myself are two totally different things." Clark shook his head.

"Hmmm. Do you wish to continue? We can remove you from the situation. Wipe their memories until this is nothing but an unpleasant dream."

"No."

"Very well then, remember the rules. Don't tell them too much about the afterlife, never use your powers to harm another, unless you want to barred from Heaven's gates, and summon me should you need help or grow weary of this … place." Her lips curled up in disgust. "Now I must go. I have to go, others to check in with."

He nodded. They definitely threw you in the deep end and expected you to learn to swim if you wanted to survive. Gone as suddenly as she came, she left Clark alone again.

Carey took her to a bar on the outskirts of town where they could blend in to the crowd. Shooters was what he liked to think of as an upper-class dive bar. They weren't fancy but the place was clean, the bathroom didn't look as if you'd catch an S.T.D from breathing the air, and the service was fast and friendly. It was the perfect place to drink in the middle of the day in nice clothing without batting an eyelash. Last thing they wanted was an audience for their forced reunion. Seated across from her at a table for two in the back, he studied her. Never in a million years would he have imagined Savannah West would grow up to be smoking hot.

Ebony tresses fell just below her shoulders. Her tall frame was slender but muscular, like Michelle Rodriguez if she'd been dipped in chocolate and gained five inches. It screwed with his head, having his cock strain against his pants for the childhood best friend who'd bailed when he needed her most. The waitress returned with a tray, setting a bucket of beer and two shots of straight whiskey on the table.

"Here you go. I'll be back to check on you two later."

"Thanks," he peered at her name tag, "Mandy."

The girl gave a muted smile. Her brown eyes darted toward a silent Savannah. He could see her mentally trying to figure out their relationship. Under other circumstances, he'd be amused.

"Of course." Mandy walked off. Savannah tossed back her shot like a pro.

"Aaah." She hissed through her teeth. "It always burns so good."

Her delicate pink tongue darted out to lick her lips.

Fuck.

He arched a brow. "Drink a lot?"

"Nope." She shook her head, sending strands of black silk flying. A layer fell into her eyes, marring her buttoned-up agent style. His mind began to form images of what she'd look like out of the black slacks and conservative button up shirt. Would her underwear be as bland? It was all too easy to see her curves highlighted in a black corset and thong.

"Gotta stay sharp and keep the reflexes up." Her answer pulled him from his lustful haze.

I seriously need to get laid. Apparently six months is too long.

"You see a lot of time in the field?" Swirling his shot glass, he watched the amber liquid shift.

"Not usually, but you know they shuffle us around like a deck of cards when necessary."

He nodded. "You have a partner though, right?"

"Yeah. Are we gonna keep bullshitting?"

"Jesus, Savannah." He pushed air out through his teeth. *So much for polite conversation.* The cold tone put a halt to the massive swelling of his cock. *Wah Wah Wah* played in his head.

"It was a simple question." She shrugged.

"It was a copout." Refusing to let her put her wall back up as though she hadn't been shaken to her core twenty minutes earlier, he called her out.

"Why?" The haughty look she issued rankled. He wanted to wipe the expression off her face. Peel back the persona she wore like a shield and retrieve the Vannah he knew still existed, held hostage inside her, like Rapunzel in her tower.

"Because you're acting like we just met." Narrowing his eyes, he leaned forward.

"No." She shook her head. "But we're not besties either. We don't know each other anymore."

"You really believe that?" The dismissive words wounded. Sure, over the years they'd changed, but *stranger*, seemed a pretty harsh label for two people who'd known each other since they were in diapers.

"You don't?" She arched an eyebrow. "You said yourself I'd changed."

"I can't work with you like this." *I don't like this new Savannah one bit.*

She rolled her eyes. "I don't even know what you're talking about."

"This is personal. I can't pretend otherwise. How can you?" he whispered.

The walls she hid behind collapsed. The dark abyss of pain visible in her deep brown orbs was a revelation.

"I have to. Emotions make you sloppy and vulnerable. If I get lost in my own head on this one, I'll be of no use to anyone. I've waited far too long to do that. Don't think for a moment this isn't ripping me to shreds on the inside. You have your way of dealing, and I have mine. I'm not saying it's right, but it gets me by."

"Vannah, that's no way to live." Gentler now that he understood, he softened his voice.

"Well, if we crack this, maybe I won't have to." She cleared her throat." Enough with the heart-to-heart. Tell me what you know."

He tossed back his shot, breathed through the trail of fire left in the whiskey's wake, and began. "Not much more than you. Clark showed up this morning like he never left. I thought I was still drunk from the night before, at first. Then I sobered, and he remained. Once he moved something and I touched him, I couldn't deny it. He mentioned you were in danger. I knew I was going to do what he said regardless, whether I was going stark-raving mad or not." She opened her mouth to speak and he shook his head. "If the position was reversed and I needed help, would you come?"

"Yeah, I would. You can't be best friends with someone for twenty-one years and forget them in ten. At least I can't."

"Exactly." He grabbed a beer from the bucket, popped the top, and slid it across to her before he opened his own.

"What did Clark say?" The anxiety in her tone wasn't lost on him.

"Not much. He said the kidnappers were back and there was a lot we didn't know. I guess it'll be coming to light soon." Trailing a finger through the condensation on the bottle, he watched the water separate to avoid the inquiring gaze looking for answers he couldn't provide.

"Did he say how or when?" Impatience sharpened her words.

He lifted the brown bottle, took a long draw, and shook his head. "He said they'd come to us."

"Oh my God, they want to finish what they started." Her eyes widened. He could see the wheels in her head spin.

"How can you know that?" he asked, unable to follow the path she'd taken to get there.

"I'm taking an educated guess. It's the only reason they'd have for coming back now—to tie loose ends. Perhaps this will allow them to complete their ritual."

"Ritual?" *How could she get all of this from a letter and a tarot card?*

"Serial killers have a variety of reasons why they kill. Some are opportunistic, where there's a driving force but no real game plan. Others have more specific requirements. They're re-enacting some trauma that happened in their life , or an ideal they wish to leave by. It may not make sense to us, because to them it's very real. Their way of righting a wrong or giving meaning to their life. ." Her tone was matter-of-fact as she spoke with an intensity that showed how much she enjoyed her job. Their conversation seemed out of place here among the popular music playing over the speakers and the trivial conversation taking place around them. College students filled the surrounding tables, drinking, chatting, and blowing off steam.

His gaze scanned the room and it hit him. They were the only somber couple here. A song with a hard-hitting bass came on and the couple beside them walked over to the tiny area designated as a dance floor. The lithe woman with cocoa skin pressed her round ass into her partner as he wrapped his arms around her waist and they moved as one to the beat.

Carey envied them. His cock stirred and he forced his mind back to the topic at hand. "You think this is one of those re-enacting cases?" he asked.

"Maybe." A thoughtful expression settled over her face. "I'll never forget that freakish clown outfit… now I wonder if it tied in to the ritual. I know they didn't travel with the carnival—the police hit a dead end with that. Perhaps the kidnappers scout out the carnivals. See where they'll be moving to and follow, ride their tailcoats." She placed her tongue in her cheek.

Releasing a sigh, he shrugged. "I don't know."

"There are all just theories, nothing concrete, but it's a start."

He was impressed. It was easy to see why she was good at what she did.

"How would you try to make a connection between what happened and other cases?"

"First I'd need to get my hands on our case file, and then I'd search using people taken from carnivals or circus acts. Perhaps it has something to do with that." Her body twitched. "I knew clowns were creepy, but I never knew they killed outside of the movies."

He couldn't say he'd watched *IT* lately. "I can get you the case files."

"Won't you get in trouble?"

Now she cares. "Being next in line for sheriff in a small town does have some perks, city slicker."

She smirked. "We don't have to play the whose-is-bigger game, Carey. I don't even have a penis." *No, but I bet your pussy is delicious.*

"Which is a good thing, considering metaphorically speaking, you trump me being F.B.I. and all."

"You know I don't see it like that. We're all law enforcement agents looking to keep the peace and gain victims justice."

"If that's true, why go for the F.B.I.?"

"Because I had my heart set on criminal profiling. I knew going through the Bureau and putting in my time was the best way to go."

"When did you know it was what you wanted to do?" Curious to know how someone went from dreaming of becoming a teacher to a federal agent, he focused in on her words, trying to read between the lines.

"After I got through with my sessions with my psychologist I started to get really into human psychology. How the mind works and what events in our past shape who we'll be. I wanted answers beyond what she could give me. I didn't like the 'sometimes bad things happen to good people' bit I was being force-fed. I wanted— no, I needed to do more." Swinging her beer toward him, she asked, "What about you? Carey Carr a cop?"

"I know, I know. When I lost Clark I just saw how pointless the stupid shit I did was. The time for teenage rebellion was gone. I dropped out of school not too long after you transferred. It just wasn't the place I needed to be. I spent a period lost, confused, and hurting. But when I pulled it together I knew I wanted to help pick up the pieces of Dale, make people feel safe again and stop wasting potential and time, you know?"

"I do. It was a mess here for awhile." His gaze shifted to the bustling bar, but his mind went back to the past. A lingering sadness had tinged everyone and everything in town the rest of the year. Parents held their children a little tighter. Kids went in when the sun went down. An unspoken curfew had been issued for teens. The campus issued a buddy system mandate and passed out pamphlets about being aware of your surroundings and how to escape an attacker, along with a rash of self-defense classes and speakers. It would help bring some comfort for others, never him.

"How long are you here for?" he asked, eager to change the subject when pain appeared in the depths of her eyes.

"Just through the weekend. I had a half day today. I'll drive back Sunday to be at work Monday."

"You staying at your parents' place?"

"Yeah, it would crush them if I didn't. Speaking of my parents, I should probably head home soon." A quick look at the bucket told him they'd worked their way through the half dozen. Any more alcohol and driving might get iffy.

"Why don't you stop by the station tomorrow and take a look at some files? Everyone knows you. It wouldn't be strange if you stopped in to chat and look over some unsolved cases. I know it's not much but it beats sitting around waiting for Clark to pop back in."

"Agreed, sounds like a plan. Any particular time?"

"I'm open. Let's exchange numbers."

He pulled out his smart phone and she followed suit. They exchanged phone numbers and he settled the tab. Out in the parking lot they paused by their cars. The soft scent of honeysuckle teased his nose. He wanted to move closer and inhale deep. Silence stretched between them, and he found himself at a loss. This was the first time they'd had a civil conversation since everything happened. It felt good. Not quite the same as before but nice nonetheless.

"You seem to like bluntness, so I'm going to come right out and ask. When this is over are you driving back off into the sunset and forgetting about me again?"

She winced. "I deserved that. No, I want to work our way back to where we once were if you're game."

"I am." He drank in her beauty. It was like an episode of The Twilight zone. Perhaps this was how it had been for Clark. The boy had been in love with her since the twelfth grade.

"Good, I'm looking forward to it." An almost shy smile graced her lips. He couldn't help the answering smile that formed. *Look at us making nice.*

"I am too, Vannah." He'd had plenty of friends over the years, male and female, but none had come close to Clark or Vannah.

Pausing with her hand on the door, she glanced over her shoulder at him. "This really happened right? We saw Clark today?"

"Unless we've both flown off the deep end at the same time, yeah, I think we did." He nodded. As the heat of the moment faded and the day came to a close, doubt crept in.

"I don't know that I believe in ghosts Carey."

"Worst-case scenario. We look into the case and come up with Zilch, right?"

"Right." She nodded.

"I'll see you tomorrow then."

He watched her until she was buckled up and drove off. You could never be too careful and to say he had an overprotective streak a mile long when it came to her would be a gross understatement. When he turned and got into his black sedan, he flinched. Clark sat in the passenger seat. His expression was stoic and his eyes stormy. *It's definitely real, Vannah.*

"You like her, don't you?" Clark asked. His lips were flattened into a straight line, and his nostrils flared.

"It's Vannah. Of course I like her."

"Yes, but its different now. I saw how you looked at her. There was nothing brotherly about it." Clark jerked his head in the direction Vannah had gone. The possessiveness made Carey want to take a step back. His mannerisms screamed, 'back off'.

Carey cleared his throat. "Clark she's gorgeous, and I'm not blind. So, yeah, I looked."

"Don't do that," he snapped.

"Do what?" Carey shook his head, lost.

"Lie to me."

"Clark, I don't even know *who* she is right now. We're two people trying to keep our heads above water."

"It's okay, Carey. If she was going to be with anyone, I'd want it to be you." His hollow tone didn't sit right.

"You're jumping the gun there—"

"No, I don't think I am. The air between the two of you practically sizzled."

"With anger." *Most of the woman's responses were hot and cold, tinged with anger or colored by pain.*

"Hmmm." The doubtful expression on Clark's face earned an eye roll.

Carey turned on the ignition and digested what his brother said. "Please don't try to play ghost matchmaker."

Clark burst into laughter. "Oh I've missed you something fierce."

"Ditto, little brother, ditto. Can you … talk about where you were?"

"No, just that I was happy and taken care of."

"That's good enough for me." There were a million questions he wanted to ask Clark but right now his brain was shot. Too much had happened in such a short amount of time. Right now his twin was back and really that was all that mattered, even if they did have their work cut out for them.

Chapter Three

She stood at the kitchen counter mixing a blend of cream and sugar in her coffee. Dressed in a pair of black sweatpants and a gray shirt from the academy, she was struck silent by how good it felt to be home. Her job was so all-encompassing that by the time she surfaced for air, long chunks of time had flown by. If her best friend didn't also work in the same office she'd be lonely indeed.

"It's good to have you home, sweetheart." Her mother padded over in a pair of pink slippers and a matching bathrobe.

"Morning, Mama. It's good to be home." Savannah bent to hug her close, inhaled the scent of soap and coconut hair product.

"Could've fooled me the way you stay away," her mother grumbled as they pulled apart.

"You know I just get caught up in my work."

Her mother pulled down a mug from the cabinet and began her own coffee routine.

"We understand how important your work is to you, Savannah. We just worry. You need more than cases in your life. They can't take care of you when you're sick, keep you company, or warm your bed."

"Mom!" Her face burned.

"What? I'm old, not dead. Besides, how do you think you got here?" She wiggled her eyebrows.

"A stork."

Her mother laughed. "I'm so glad you got my sense of humor."

Savannah leaned in. "Me too," she whispered.

Footfalls sounded on the stairs, and a few moments later her father entered the room. The Ex-Navy man was tall and slender with silver hair cropped close to his head and skin the color of warm syrup. Retired, he worked at the V.A. Hospital.

"There's my June bug."

"Hi Daddy." She placed her mug on the counter and moved over to hug him. He surrounded her with his arms and rubbed her arm before he stepped back.

"Good to have you home. How's work?"

"It's good, Dad."

"Oh Lord, I thought we agreed to put that talk on the back burner." Her mother placed her hands on her hips, and narrowed her eyes.

"What? I was just asking her how things were going, Seleste." His eyes sparkled with mirth. Her mom had been at him for years about leaving his work at the door. Now that the argument extended to Savannah he loved giving her a hard time.

"MMhmm. Let me get my coffee before you two drive my blood pressure through the roof." Her mother turned and picked up the mug, taking a sip.

"Woman, your blood pressure is fine. You do yoga every day and shovel that leafy green stuff down both our throats like it's going out of style."

Their playful banter made Savannah smile. *I've missed this.*

"Hmph. What are your plans for today?" her mother asked.

"I'm actually getting together with Carey Carr at the police station. He's going to show me around."

The atmosphere went from light to heavy.

"We ran into each other yesterday, buried the hatchet so to speak, and caught up. It bothered me the way I'd left things, so … we're trying to move forward." She kept her eyes glued to the light brown liquid in her cup, refusing to look up as their gazes burned a hole in her.

"That's good, Savannah," her mom whispered.

"Thanks, I wanted you to hear it from me and not someone else. Good news travels fast in this town." She rolled her eyes.

"I'm proud of you. I know that wasn't easy to do." The compassion in her father's eyes humbled her.

"Thank you, Daddy."

"Why don't you two go sit at the table while I get breakfast started?"

"You sure you don't need any help?" Savannah asked.

"No, I'll be fine, and your father wants to talk shop, I'm sure."

Savannah smiled. "All right then, come on Daddy, let's go get shop-talk out of system." They walked out of the cozy kitchen into the dining room and sank down on the maple-colored chairs.

"So tell me how you're really doing." The ex J.A.G. member knew all too well how much you brought the job home with you.

"I'm good, really."

He stared into her eyes for few moments and nodded, pleased by whatever it was he'd found. "Excellent, now feed me some harmless morsels."

As they talked she could almost allow herself to forget the danger that lurked around the corner, making every second spent with her parents more precious. She'd cheated death the first time. Chances were they'd go through elaborate lengths to make sure she didn't escape again. The normalcy was the quiet before the storm she prayed she was strong enough to survive.

Dressed in a pair of gray slacks and a light blue scoop-neck top, she sat outside of the police station and texted Carey. *I'm out front.*

Her heart beat faster than normal, and her mouth went dry. Elephants stampeded inside her tummy. She'd passed the point of butterflies the minute she stepped foot outside the door on the way there. She did her best to convince herself it had nothing to do with

Carey. *I was never really good at lying to myself. If only the boys at work could see me now, losing my cool over a man. A sexy man with a body made for sin, tattoos I want to trace with my tongue, and a past that's bonded us for life.* She played things by the book and made justice her reason for moving mountains to solve cases. It earned her the moniker Sheriff West, which stuck. Lust had no place here.

Her phone buzzed. She glanced down at the display screen.

I'm coming out to get you. Her pussy grew moist. Apparently her body had other plans.

She stepped out of the car, pocketed her phone, and mentally put on her armor. *Damn.* Carey was a vision in black as he walked toward her. The shirt highlighted his broad shoulders and the plain black pants featured the round, firm ass, her hand itched to squeeze and fondle. She drank in the sergeant chevrons and badge. Seeing the reformed bad boy in a uniform took her breath away. Desire simmered in her belly.

Ashamed, she glanced down. *How can I be attracted to Carey? It's the ultimate kick to the nuts to Clark's memory.* Guilt weighed her like an anchor.

"Hey, you made it." He smiled.

"You doubted?"

"A little. I think a part of me was still waiting to wake up and find this was some alcohol-induced dream, and no, I don't get plastered often."

"You don't have to explain, Carey. I know what yesterday was."

"Yeah… you ready to go in?"

She adjusted the strap to her satchel. "Did you tell them I was coming?"

"Yeah, I did. Once I mentioned your name nothing else I said afterward was heard."

"That'll probably work to our advantage."

"Yes and no."

"What are you trying to say?"

"They're excited, Savannah. They want to talk to you, congratulate you on your success. I told them not to crowd you too much, but you know Dale."

She closed her eyes. This was a long time coming. The prodigal daughter had returned and for once she was interacting, not holed up in the house. "I expected as much."

"Are you going to play nice?" Carey's concerned expression made her snort. His haughty tone doused the flames of wanting.

"I'm not a total asshole, Carey."

"Hey, I'm just looking out for my people. They don't deserve any disrespect or alienation."

"I know better than to piss in someone else's pond."

His eyes lightened in the sun, turning to a brilliant blue that matched the sadness she saw reflected in the oceanic pools. "This used to be your pond too."

The guilt trip triggered her ire. "Are you going to throw stones in a glass house?" Her voice was cool and calm. But on the inside she seethed, ready to rip into him and deliver hurt, have him feel the pain he carelessly inflicted.

"Hey! I stayed." he barked. Anger tightened his muscles. His chest stuck out, and his strong jaw clenched.

"You had your turbulent times too. Why should I be the bad guy because I didn't rage out loud in actions or words?" She counted to ten. "Listen, we're not going to get anywhere being at each other's throats."

He sighed. "You're right. This is petty. I'll be nice, if you're nice."

"Deal."

"We should go inside. I'm sure they're all watching us." He turned on his heel and she followed. Reality hit her like a sledgehammer. She was going to see all the gory details up close and in person.

Can I keep it together? Look at this the same way I would any other case? The pressure pushed down on her. Every step she took became harder than the one previous. A fine sheen of sweat broke out on her forehead. He opened the door to the station, holding it open as she walked inside the mid-sized brick building. The short hallway gave way to a homey atmosphere. The small desk boasted two computers manned by a burly officer with dark brown skin, a bald head, and a husky build.

"Sergeant, Agent West."

"Savannah, this is Officer Williams."

She walked over to the desk and offered her hand. "Nice to meet you, Officer Williams."

They shook. His grip was firm and his hand steady.

"Likewise." He measured her with an assessing gaze.

She stepped back, pulled her ID badge off her belt, and set it on the counter. "I know it's a technicality, but here's my information to check me in."

Officer Williams smiled. *Looks like I passed the test.* His fingers flew over the keys as he logged in her information.

"You're all set, Agent West."

"Excellent. Thank you."

"Come on, I'll show you the rest of the place."

A few yards away they entered the workspace. Six wooden desks sat in rows of three on a linoleum floor. A couple of offices sat off to the side in the back. Two of the six desks were occupied. A few faces were vaguely familiar.

"You remember Officer Adam and Officer Varney. They went to school with us." The tow-haired, tall man with pale skin and the man with chin–length, dark hair had been in her classes from the time she was in kindergarten.

"Nice to see you again." She gave a polite smile.

"Same here. Congratulations on your success," Adams said.

"We're proud of you here in Dale." Varney grinned. The sincerity in the kind words warmed her. One of the perks of small-town living was when one of the town members made good, the whole town felt as if they were a part of it.

"Thank you." She flashed a smile.

"Officer Rodriguez and Officer Nolan are new additions. You'll meet them later. Chief's out of the office for the next couple of days, but I'll take you into mine."

She followed him over to the smaller office on the opposite side of the room.

"Welcome to my office." The mid-sized room boasted a black desk with a name tag, two chairs, and a filing cabinet. "Have a seat."

She sank into the seat and he circled the desk, pulling a key from his pocket. Sitting down, he unlocked his desk drawer. He removed a manila file, placing it on top of the desk.

"Are you sure you're ready for this?" His face softened and he lowered his voice.

Gulping, she braced herself. "As ready as I could ever be."

"Is this the first time you've seen the file?"

The abundance of compassion made her squirm. If this continued she wouldn't be able to get through it. "Yes."

"Do you want to be alone?"

"No. You're fine. This has to be done correctly. I'll make sure that happens." *With you here the chances of tears is much less. I'm not about to be some blubbering mess in front of you.*

Her hands were clammy. The file felt cool in her hands, like Clark. The impossibility of the situation had her reeling. Taking a deep breath, she put a tight grip on the meltdown lurking just around the corner in her head and prepared for the gruesome sight that awaited her.

She peeled open the folder, ignored the pictures gathered at the back with a paper clip. Glancing at the General Report she read. Savannah M. West. Words she could handle. *Be objective.* The generic jargon listing cause of death, suspected motives, and eye witness reports told her more of what she all ready knew.

Coroner's Report. Tension flooded her body. Her mouth salivated. She sucked in air through her nostrils and let it out slow. Heart was removed from the body by a jagged instrument pre mortem. Wings carved onto the back of his skin with a precise instrument, like a scalpel. Interlocked symbols representing the male and female were carved into his wrist.

Jesus Clark, what did these bastards do to you?" The imagery tugged at her brain, but she couldn't focus. It was like a snowball rolling downhill. Now that she started on the file, she had to finish, and that meant viewing everything.

Carey felt like a peeping Tom. The emotions that crossed Savannahs' face were powerful. Grief poured off her in oppressive waves, its tendrils reaching out in an attempt to ensnare, wrap up him up in its binding grip. He pushed back from his desk and walked to the window. Peering out at nothing, he regulated his breathing. Automatically his mind began to replay that night. The same way it always did.

Summer, 2001
"Savannah and I are going to the carnival tonight. Do you want to go?"

Carey looked up at his brother from his twin bed and smiled. *How could he be so clueless?* The way Savannah looked at him was not sisterly. Perhaps if he gave them some time alone nature would take its course. God knew Clark talked about how he felt enough.

"No, I think I'll hang back here. See if there's a party going." *Give you a chance to make your move.*

Clark sighed. "More partying?" The disappointment in his voice stung. It wasn't like his brother to judge.

"What?" Carey placed his hands behind his head on the bed. "We're only going to be young and free once."

"Yes, but some mistakes can follow you for a lifetime." Clark stood from the desk and grabbed the jacket he had draped over the back of his chair.

"Really, Clark? You preaching to me now?" He rolled his eyes.

"No, just stating the obvious." Clark pulled on a brown leather jacket over his shirt. It got cold here at night.

"Noted, but I'm fine."

"Your grades say otherwise."

The matter-of-fact statement raised his hackles. *It's not like I'm failing everything.*

"Come on, math was never my best subject. I can make it up later."

"You need to get a handle on your partying and buckle down."

"Since when did you become such a stick in the mud?" Carey sat up in bed, disgusted. "Look. You do what makes you happy and I'll do the same. You're the golden boy. Be happy with the title and leave me alone." Last thing he wanted to be was their father's yes man. *I'm out of the house and I'm going to explore everything denied me before. Deal with it.*

"Why do you always say that?" Clark snapped. "We're equals."

"You actually believe that, don't you?" Carey shook his head. "At the end of the day I'm going to be me. You need to focus on what's right in front of you before you lose it." Swinging his legs off the bed, he rose.

"What's that supposed to mean?" Clark frowned.

"Think about it. You'll figure it out." He grabbed his keys off the dresser and walked out the door, laughing at the confused expression Clark wore. For being so smart he was missing the obvious.

Present

"I think I've found some important clues I can work with."

He spun around. Her eyes were glossy. Yet, she managed to hold it together.

"What do you need from me?"

"Copies are out I know, so just let me take notes. Have you seen these files?"

"Yeah... too many times." He pulled the file out periodically and kept a constant lookout for any similar activity.

"These markings and the removal of the heart mean *something*." She scrunched her face up as if she'd tasted a bitter beer. "I can't figure out what though. I'm going to plug them into the computer and see what I can come up with."

"What do you think about the heart being missing?" *Other then the fact that they were sick bastards.*

"Honestly... I think they kept it as a souvenir. It's not uncommon for these people to keep a memento they can look at and re-live the moment." Her voice wavered.

He was grateful for the show of emotions. It confirmed below the surface of her cool, calm exterior, things were happening.

She picked up her satchel, opened the flap, stuck her hand inside, and froze. "Shit."

"What's wrong?"

"I forgot to open this yesterday." She pulled out a small, manila envelope. "Give me a second?"

"Sure." He walked away from the window and sank into the chair on the opposite side of his desk. She opened the envelope gingerly and pulled out an item wrapped in red tissue paper and a white card with a giant red heart on the front.

"Get fan mail often?" Carey asked smugly.

"You'd be surprised." She shook her head. "There are a lot of loose cannons out there."

She opened the card. The wry smile slid from her face. Her body tensed.

"What's wrong?" *What the hell was in that letter?*

"It's them." The mild tremor in her voice terrified him. Clearly it took a lot to rattle this woman.

"Who?" It was a struggle to keep his voice even. *What Clark said would happen is. They've brought the fight to us.* The psychic ghost phenomena made him shiver.

"The killers."

"What!" He stood and hurried around the desk to peer over her shoulder .

"I need gloves. Now." The mutter was more to herself than him as he read the letter over her shoulder.

> Dear Agent West,
>
> Last we met you had the sweet bloom of first love all over you, and we knew then and there we had to have a little taste. But you got away. Split our perfect puzzle piece into two. We never forgot you. Imagine our surprise seeing you all grown up and hunting our brethren. It must've been destiny. We are slaves to fate in all things. It's so freeing to cast the cards and follow your path to greatness.
>
> Now is the time we choose to step from the shadows and claim the masterpieces we've created. It's been a long, fun journey and soon it'll be complete. Let's play a game of who can find who first. We'll be seeing you soon, Agent West. I assure you this time you won't get away.

"Fuck! We need our people on this now." After all this time they'd reached out to her! Alarm bells rang in his head. The letter's words smacked of stalking. The thought of them watching her undetected for any amount of time made him want to go ape-shit. Too close and right on the heels of his brother's magic re-appearing trick.

"No. I want to examine this thing from top to bottom before we get anyone in on it." She set her jaw and stared him down.

"Vannah." His protests died when he saw the determination on her face and the fire that burned bright in her eyes. He'd pry that envelope from her hands if he had to.

No, gaining control of the situation wouldn't be worth the friction it'd cause. She knew what she was doing, and her finger prints were all ready on it, so technically the evidence was already tampered with.

"This is personal." She turned to her bag, dug inside, and came out with a pair of gloves.

"You carry them around with you?" He snickered. The noise eased the tension rapidly gathering like a storm.

"This *is* my work bag." The pop of latex made him grit his teeth. She worked the blue gloves onto her hand and carefully peeled back the layers of tissue. Rustles filled the air. Time slowed. He held his breath when the last piece was removed.

"A card?" he asked. *Was this a prank?*

"A Tarot Card."

She straightened, dug in her bag once more, and produced a small, gray voice recorder. Bending over the card without further disturbing it, she pressed play.

"The suspects have sent me a Tarot Card, the Lovers. The interlocked male and female on the card have been personalized. He's acquired pictures of his victims, Clark Carr and Savannah West, cut out their faces, and placed them on the male and female at the bottom of the card. The winged, angel-like creature with the body of a female and wings has had its face blacked out. Possibly, because it represents Clark, or because they hate love and females. At first glance I can't tell if anything else has been altered. We'll have to locate an original and compare. The removal of Clark's heart makes sense now, because I got away. The note within the package tells me the Killers have been doing this a long time. I wouldn't be surprised if their murders match the same amount of cards in the tarot deck." She clicked pause.

He was impressed by her ability to compartmentalize. Despite the mental anguish she had to be going through, she remained professional. Her face was a mask of concentration and her eyes blazed with intensity and passion. *I see why they call her Sheriff West. I wouldn't want to be placed on the wrong end of her gun.*

"We need to call my people and see how they'd like to proceed. I know this is your jurisdiction, but it was sent to me personally. I'm going to request they let me proceed from here."

"Do you think they'll agree?" Everything hinged on her answer.

"I can be persuasive."

Okay that was kind of hot... in a scary, not-to-be-messed-with, woman kind of way.

"I get the feeling this isn't going to be their last present. They'll want to recreate that event, which means returning to Dale."

"Why would they risk it?"

"Because it's their last hurrah. Getting caught is irrelevant. Completing their masterpiece is what matters."

"I don't get that."

"These killings are their life's purpose. The same way we feel about our jobs and bringing justice is the way they feel about murder... I'm just not sure why yet."

"What do you need to figure it out?"

"Time, analysis... more information. I've already begun to draw up a profile, but I need to dig deeper, search the database to see if I can get any hits on similar murders."

"You think you see a pattern?"

"They talked a lot about fortune... I see a white male. Two actually. Close, maybe even family members. They'd need to have near identical upbringings. This obsession with the Tarot is very strange, even by my standards."

"That's not reassuring."

"It wasn't meant to be. It's a ticking time bomb. We need to defuse before it explodes."

"What's the first step?"

"I'll call my people." She pushed away from the table. "I know this goes without saying, but don't let anyone touch this." She dug her phone from her Mary Poppins bag on the counter. "I'm going to take this outside."

He nodded and watched her leave. "Clark, I don't know if you can hear me, but I could use some guidance right now."

"Hey."

Carey jumped. Clark stood to his right. "Can't you give a warning or something?" Ghost Clark creeped him out slightly. The apprehension made him feel bad. *Come on, it's my brother.*

"Like what? The whole angel and bell thing is a myth."

"So you're an angel?"Awe filled him as he studied the face similar to his, but frozen in time.

"Uh-uh." Clark shook his finger. "I can't go into details. I was just using that reference as an example."

"Why can't you talk about anything?" He frowned. *Sounds suspect. Had he gone rogue to do this? Risked being banished from the afterlife?*

"You aren't meant to know too much." Clark looked up. "They don't like it. Change the subject or this will be cut short."

"I don't know what to do with Savannah." He ran a hand over his face.

"Umm... help her solve this case." The expression on Clark's face said *duh.*

"Obviously. I mean how to act. She's putting up a great front, but I know she's hurting. Do I treat her strictly as a partner or as a friend? We're walking very narrow lines here."

"What do you think?" Clark tilted his head.

"I think she'll always be Vannah to me. However, I don't want to piss her off. If I did something to jeopardize this investigation, I wouldn't be able to live with myself."

"Sometimes you have to rock the boat to get where you need to be." Easy to say when you weren't the one doing the rocking.

Oka,y Buddha. "I asked for advice not cryptic comments."

Clark sighed. "She needs to be challenged."

"Have you seen the guns on her these days?"

Clark laughed. "Are you going to tell me you're scared of Vannah?"

"I'm not, but my penis is. She looks like the kind to bring you to your knees with a strategically placed kick, followed by a right hook. My balls hurt just thinking about it."

All humor faded. "She'd never hurt you, Carey." His fast-paced switch of gears made Carey wary. To have been dead for so long, he seemed to know a lot.

"How can you know that? I need an answer of substance this time. Because the whole cloak and dagger bit is getting old, and not helping me whatsoever.

"I can see through to heart."

The words rang true. "You always could," Carey whispered. The two had an uncanny connection that kept them on the same page more often than not. It reminded him of the link they possessed as twins.

"You could too if you tried," Clark insisted.

Carey snorted. "I might be in a uniform, but I still crash and burn in every relationship I attempt."

"Maybe because they weren't the right women."

"Oh no, trust me, they were right." He smiled at the memories.

"Maybe to the small head in your pants."

"Damn, all this time and you're still a buzz kill." Carey grinned. The familiar banter was a balm to his fractured soul. He'd never felt right... whole since Clark died.

"And you're still hard-headed and stubborn."

"That was a trait we both shared."

Clark smiled. "I know, but I choose to use mine for good."

"Boring." His singsong voice took him back to childhood. "I've missed you so much, Clark." When he left the mystic behind it was almost like old times. Not that he could ever forget he was dead.

"I know." Clark placed a hand on his shoulder.

"After this is done I'll never see you again, will I?" he whispered.

"Not for a long, long time."

Carey nodded.

"I have to go, but remember this. The old Vannah is still in there. She needs to tap back into that. Remember who she was, and who we were."

"I don't understand what that has to do with this case."

"Trust me?"

"Always."

"Then do whatever you need to do to make that happen, Carey. The men after you are some of the worst evil I've seen."

The words made him slightly sick to his stomach.

"I'm not sure… there are things I can't remember. Bad memories they took away when I crossed over. So I wouldn't have to bear the burden. "

"It's okay, Clark. I'm glad you don't remember. You shouldn't have to." He placed a hand on his brother's shoulder to reassure him.

Clark cast a longing gaze at the door.

"You can wait until she comes back," Carey said.

"Why? She won't even look at me." Clark glanced down.

"You know why. Don't you?" Carey hunched down, forcing his brother to look up. *This is the least I can do for him.*

"Guilt."

"Oh brother, you still haven't seen what was right in front of you. She loved you, Clark."

"W-what? No… she couldn't have." His eyes were as round as bowling balls. .

"Yes, Savannah Marie West is so in love with you it's disgusting."

"Is?" Clark looked almost hopeful.

"There hasn't been anyone else, Clark."

"What!"

Now he's getting it. "She's been single this entire time as far as I can tell."

"Bullshit." Clark stepped away.

"Why don't you ask her yourself?"

"Now is not the time!"

"Not the time for what?" Savannah asked.

46

They turned as one in that way they had mastered from the moment they came from the womb.

"To… get personal," Carey covered.

"What's going on here?" Savannah crossed her arms beneath her breasts and frowned.

"Just twin talk," Clark said.

"Why do I feel like you're lying?" The unimpressed expression on her face was all too familiar.

You wanted her to look at you, little brother. She's definitely doing that now.

"I—we—things between us are just so unfinished." Clark stumbled over his words like an adorable high-schooler talking to his first crush.

Savannah ducked her head. "Yeah, they are."

"Later?" Clark whispered. The unspoken communication that passed between them humbled Carey. *This is what true love looks like.* Even after all this time they operated on the same wavelength. Her normally cold eyes were warm and her body language had changed entirely. All it took to make her remember the good times was Clark. Carey could just step out of the equation altogether. The thought smarted.

"Yes… its time." Savannah looked up. All traces of vulnerability were smoothed back into the emotionless mask she wore. "But now we get the ball rolling. I have control over the operation at the moment. My people agree staying here is in the best interest of the case. Since I'm their point of contact, I have leave. It goes without saying. One whiff of emotional compromise, and I'll be yanked off this thing faster than you can bat an eye."

"Where do we start?" Carey asked.

"Show me to the lab. The proper paperwork is being typed up. They should be calling your Captain."

"That's my cue. I'll be around." Clark disappeared once more.

"I don't think I'm ever going to get used to that." Carey shook his head. Just when he adapted to Clark's return, he pulled a stunt like that and he was straddling the line between freaked out and happy to have his brother back.

"Yeah, me either." The visible pain was washed away when she blinked.

The three of them were the walking wounded. It was time they received closure in more ways than catching a killer.

Clark left them but the apprehension stayed. He'd petitioned for this, the right to come back and guide them now that the killers were back. Hanging on to your past was frowned upon. It kept you from fully assimilating and leaving behind earthly things.

He figured Carey and Vannah must be pretty important for them to even care. Lives weren't predestined the way people thought. Free will cut short plans. Warped and changed the best-laid paths. It was rare that they'd step in and change the course of things. He wanted to know more, but it was one of the stipulations of returning. As were keeping his mouth closed about the afterlife and remaining in the dark about what was going on. The temptation to alter things might be too great.

He ran a hand through his hair.

It was lonely here in the in-between. Most spirits who lingered around these parts were angry or worse, dark. He missed his friends. *Think of it as being a secret agent.* The concept did nothing to ease his pain. Vannah was even more beautiful than he remembered her. The gangly limbs of youth had gained curves. Her round face had slimmed and matured. It was very different from the one he remembered. He'd wasted all the time hiding his feelings because he was terrified he'd ruin their friendship. Today, he'd do anything to go back and tell her. *The next time we're alone together, I'll come clean.*

Decision made, he shoved his hands into his pockets and wandered into the twilight.

Chapter Four

Savannah blinked, wincing at the gritty feel of sand behind her lids. She'd been scouring over the databases and come up empty-handed. The search was still too broad. *Time to take a break.*

Since she'd officially reopened the case they'd set her up in Carey's office. Being confined in a small space with him was strange. It wasn't a situation she was prepared for. In one swoop she'd gone from running away from Carey and Clark to running beside them.

Clark. Even as an apparition he had the same effect on her. Caring, sensitive, and quirky, the man—ghost—whatever the hell he was made her melt. Her body didn't seem to differentiate the difference between alive and not, and the constant arousal was driving her to distraction. Frustrated, she pushed away from the desk.

"You okay?" Carey's concerned voice caressed her in places long-ignored. Her self-imposed celibacy was on shaky ground.

"Yeah, I just need," she gestured toward the door, "air."

"Sure, take your time. You've been at the computer for a while. Why don't you pack it in for the night?"

A glance down at the black sports watch on her wrist told her it was almost midnight. Keeping things simple, she'd told her parents she had a case in Dale she couldn't talk to them about. No sense in forcing them to relive the horror a second earlier than they had to. They seemed excited to have her home for a bit, and were respectful of her wishes. Though she hated to admit it, it was nice having the both of best worlds. Family closeby and her job.

"You know what? I think I will." Closing out of the databases, she logged out, locked her computer, and shut it down. "I'll see you tomorrow morning."

"Come in late. You look like you could use some sleep."

Inside, the words made her flinch. No woman wanted to hear she looked like shit. On the outside she smiled.

"We'll see." She lifted her bag from across the back of her chair, placed it over her shoulders, and left.

She waved at Rodriguez who was manning the front desk.

"You out of here for the night?" the caramel skinned woman asked.

"Yep."

"Have a good one."

"You too." Fifteen minutes later she was in her bedroom stripping off her sports coat and draping it on the arm of her computer chair.

"Vannah?"

The soft spoken words startled her. She spun to face a bashful-looking Clark. Her hormones surged and she silently cursed her biological make-up. Technically he was still twenty-on,e which made her a bit of a cougar. The thought thrilled her instead of dissuaded. *Fuck.*

"Clark." Awkwardness set in and she shifted her weight. "H-How are you?" She forced herself to look at him, boxing with the urge to look away. Seeing him still felt wrong, and interacting with him made her feel a bit crazy. It wasn't so bad when Carey was there to act as a buffer. The irony of the role reversal didn't escape her. Carey had never been the one she went to for comfort or understanding.

"I've been better."

The hint of sadness she picked up on cut through her internal cluster-fuck. He'd suffered atrocities straight out of *Saw* in life, only to come back to warn them and be tortured in the process.

"What's wrong?" Whatever form he took he was still Clark, her best friend and the potential love of her life that got away. She couldn't let him bleed out if she could patch the wound. She walked over to stand beside the six-foot-one male. Reaching out a hand, she stopped millimeters from touching his arm, snatching it back before it made contact. *Can I even touch him?*

"We've left things unsaid between us for far too long."

No, please don't do thi,s Clark. It'll make your leaving even more painful.

"Don't."

"I'm sorry, Savannah. I have to." *He used my full name— he isn't going to back down.*

"Go ahead. I'm listening."

"There were things I kept from you, Vannah. I was afraid."

"Why? You were my best friend. Nothing you said would've made me see you any differently."

"Don't be so sure."

"Clark. You're scaring me."

He gave her a small smile, ran a finger down the side of her face. The touch was real albeit a little cool. She closed her eyes, leaned into savor the feel of his flesh against her own with a chill that had nothing to do with temperature. She opened her eyes only to be snared by the blue-green jewels full to the brim with emotion. *This is so wrong.*

"I love you."

Her mouth flopped open and closed. "Wait—what?"

"I should've told you back then. I hid it for years. Played the best friend when what I wanted to be was your everything, I knew we were meant to be after your eighteenth birthday. You were wearing this peach dress that stopped at your knees. It took my breath away. Jason Mclaren was giving you the eye the whole party. The minute you turned your attention to someone else I took him aside and pretty much told him if he even tried to talk to you Carey and I would make his life … unpleasant."

"Clark," she gasped. Her pulse raced. Joy bubbled to the surface like the fizz in soda.

"You stole my heart somewhere along the way growing up. I could never give it to another. Who could be a better match for me, Savannah? We finished each other's sentences. Didn't hide a thing from one another. It was a rarity that I took for granted. I just… I didn't want to risk losing what we had."

"I felt the same." Her admission lifted the heavy boulder off her chest.

"Felt?"

The wounded expression that crossed his face cracked open a door inside she'd chained shut. She closed the inches of space that divided them and cupped his cool face in her hand. "I will always love you, Clark. You and I were soul-deep. When you were gone I became a piece of driftwood lost in the ocean of life. I had to rebuild myself from the ground up. I hurt a lot of people that way but it was what I had to do to survive. Now you're back and I can't help but wonder what I'm going to do when you're leave." Her voice cracked. Her bottom lip quivered.

"How can we miss out on a second opportunity because of fear? That's what robbed us in the first place."

She pulled away. "What do you want me to do?" *It seemed wrong to say "when you're dead". Yet the words spun around in her head.*

Her phone rang out like the ding of a bell ending the round of a prizefight.

"I have to get that."

"Yeah." Clark stepped back and released a deep breath. As he paced the length of the room, his nervous energy set her on edge.

She picked up the phone. "Speak."

"Jeez. You need sleep more than I thought."

"Carey?"

"I just wanted to make sure you got home okay."

Her anger melted away. "I'm fine. It's like a ten-minute drive."

"I know, but you didn't seem right tonight."

"Nothing sleep won't cure."

"You sure?"

"Positive."

"Then I'll let you go."

"Thank you, Carey."

"Any time, Vannah Banana."

He hung up before she could scold him, and she smiled.

"Carey?" Clark asked.

"Yeah. He wanted to make sure I got home okay."

"How nice of him."

There was an edge to his words. "Clark?"

"I have to go—" He disappeared before she could say more.

"Fuck." She placed her head in her hands. Carey saved her from making a horrible mistake. *A few seconds longer and I would be making out with a ghost. What the hell was I thinking?* There was no future for them. No silver lining, or happily-ever-after. This whole thing was a mind-screw.*I have to stay composed.* She removed the rest of her clothes, slipped on an oversized shirt, and sank n to the edge of her bed, unable to sleep yet. Thoughts chased each other. The emotional overload endangered all the hard work she'd put in over the years. She had a system that worked. Her heart was protected, and her life ran smoothly. Clark threatened her life like a wrecking ball. Frustrated, she turned to the solace she could always count on, work.

So much for an early night. With sleep no longer an option, she got to her feet and zombie-shuffled to her desk. Taking out a sheet of loose-leaf and a pencil, she began an old-school bubble map of thoughts. She put main points in circles and branched out with lines and more encircled thoughts. The page began to fill with random threads of concepts. None felt right.

"You are slippery sons of bitches, aren't you?" she mumbled. They were smart. She had to give them that. It made her apprehensive. People like this always had a trick up their sleeves, booby traps, or diversions. It wasn't your average case.

She didn't want any more people hurt. *The devil's in the details.* The phrase always helped her dig deep beneath the obvious. The Tarot was the key, but she only had one card to work with. They'd tracked down the specific set of cards, scanned each one for differences, and came up empty-handed. A search for bodies found with carvings etched into them had been started. But they were still sifting through the piles. To make matters worse she *knew* the killers were watching, circling the area like buzzards waiting for an animal to drop.

She pushed the ages aside, and pulled out the Tarot Cards she'd purchased to study at home. It was breaking her rules, bringing her work home, never coming up for air. Yet, there was a sense of urgency she couldn't ignore. As she studied The Lover's card, the morgue report rushed back. The interlocked female and male symbols were the key. They were on the Tarot.

Excited, she snatched up the card. The symbols were in direct correlation. It would still take some time to go over the cards, pick out key symbols, one by one, but it had narrowed the choices significantly. It felt good to make progress on this case. The fact that it distracted her from the mess with Clark was an added bonus.

That was stupid. Clark blew out a breath as he paced the length of Carey's apartment. *What had he hoped to accomplish?* He thought knowing how she felt would make him feel better in some way, give him closure.

He was wrong. Now he was jealous of Carey over nothing. The

lock sounded in the door. He tensed. *Speak of the devil, or think in this case.* The door swung open and Carey paused.

"Hi. You look upset," Carey said.

"I am."

"Okay." Carey stepped in, shut the door and locked it behind him. "What's up?" He let his bag fall to the door and shed his utility belt, carrying it with him to the couch. He set it on the cushion beside him. "I'm all ears."

"I went to see Vannah."

Carey cringed. "Didn't go well?"

"No. Sort of." He shook his head." Hell, I don't even know." He snickered at his absurdity.

"What?" Carey laughed. "Why don't you tell me the whole story?"

He relayed the events as Carey listened without commenting. It felt good to share again with his twin. Carey was the only person he'd never felt judgment from. Even when they butted heads, eventually they hashed things out.

"You guys are so ass backward." Carey shook his head." I'm not surprised she felt the same way about you. It's why I didn't go that night."

"You knew?" He turned to his brother, shocked.

"She didn't tell me, if that's what you mean. I suspected. It was written all over her face every time she looked at you when you weren't watching."

"What? Why didn't you tell me?"

Carey shrugged. "I didn't think it was my place to say. I mean, if she wanted to keep it to herself, who was I to blow her cover?"

Clark sighed. "I should've kept my mouth shut."

"I don't think so. It seems like your being back is all about unfinished business. If you hadn't told her, you'd still feel there were things left unsaid wouldn't you."

Clark blinked. "I never thought of it that way."

"That's why you have me." Carey wagged his eyebrows and

tapped the side of his head. "Other half of your brain and all that."

The revelation his words brought was a light in the darkness. It all made sense. He was sent heer to tie all the loose ends keeping him bound to Earth. Despite all the other side had to offer.

"You're absolutely right. Even when I was… there I couldn't let go of this life completely. That's why they did this."

"Is that abnormal?" Carey's eyes were full of interest.

"Very. But it does happen. Especially instances of true evil."

"So the powers that be do even things out."

Clark remained silent, unsure if answering would be breaking the rules.

"Yeah, I know you can't go into details." He rolled his eyes.

"Exactly. What do I do next?" He walked over and sat on the opposite side of the couch, facing Carey.

"I don't know. The two of you will have to figure that one out together." Carey shook his head.

"Come on, Carey! That's a copout answer, and you know it."

"It's not. You're placing me in an awkward position. The choices you make will affect the two of you for a long time to come. You have to decide what you can live with. What she could live with."

He understood the message. *Let her go.* He wasn't sure he could. Too much time spent thinking about her made him selfish. "Okay, fair enough. Tell me this, what would you do if you were me?"

"I don't know. I'm shit with relationships, and we both know Vannah isn't just some girl."

"She's so different. It's hard to read her."

Carey nodded in agreement. "Turning into an ice maiden was how she coped, I think."

"We *have* to make her remember who she was. I refuse to let her stay like this. "

"Exactly how do you expect to accomplish that? I'm curious because I tried to have a meaningful conversation with her and she pretty much bit my head off."

"With your help."

"Hey." Carey held his hands up. "Don't drag me into this too deep. I have to work with the woman on the daily. "

"Come on, man, consider it my dying wish."

"That's a low blow."

"It's true."

Carey growled. "What do you want me to do?"

"Get to know her. Underneath the front she puts up is the girl we grew up with. I see her when she lets her guard down." *I need to take a knee, accept the runner-up prize. Her being with Carey is as close to being with her as I can get.*

"You would see that. You were always the one she turned to. I'm grasping at straws."

"And now that I can't be that person you have to. She's missing out on what life's all about, Carey. There's so much pain locked away inside her. If she can just let go, I think she'd begin to heal."

"Clark , I'm not some sort of emotion whisperer."

"I know." He looked Carey in the eyes. "But you *can* do this."

"Damn you, Clark." Carey sighed. "Fine."

Clark's tense muscles relaxed. "If I know you two will be taking care of one another when my time comes again, I'll be able to go."

The look of discomfort that crossed Carey's face made Clark feel like shit. It was a lot to ask but he needed some hope to help ease the pain that came with the thought of leaving them behind once more.

Chapter Five

The sound of her phone jerked her from the heavy sleep she was loathe to leave behind. Savannah pried open her scratchy eyes and stuck her hand out of the blanket. She felt around for the device she'd set on her dresser. Finding it, she pulled it inside her cocoon.

"Hello." Her throat felt raw, and her eyes burned.

"Vannah?"

"Carey?"

"Yeah. I hate to wake you like this when I'm the one who told you to get some rest, but this can't wait."

"What happened?" She swallowed, focusing on his voice as she struggled against the stranglehold of sleep.

"You got another package."

The words made her gasp. "They know I'm here." *And I thought this case couldn't get any more personal. Murphy's law strikes again.*

"It looks that way."

"They're watching me. This isn't good. They are actively hunting."

"How can you sound so calm?"

"Because panicking isn't an option right now. I need a squad car monitoring my house. I have to tell my parents about this. Their safety is compromised." She made a mental list and began to run down each item.

"You think they'd come to your house?"

"If they thought it was necessary, yes. I put nothing past these people. It bothers me I don't know how long they've been observing. I'd wager not too long. Their letter suggested my occupation was a recent discovery."

"I'll talk to the Chief and get it started."

"Thank you. I'm getting up and coming in now. Have you opened the package?"

"Only to have the bomb experts examine it."

"Good, keep the vultures in the office away from it."

He chuckled. "You got it, Sherieff."

"Don—" The dial tone was her only response. "That little shit hung up on me!" A smirk twitched her lips upward. She pushed the covers off her body and escaped her warm nest. The wood floor was cool on her bare feet. She hissed.

The sun was just beginning to rise, so it couldn't be much more than seven. The hushed whispers of her parents and clanks of pots and pans being moved around told her she'd caught them before they started their day. She made her way down the stairs and into the kitchen where they stood at the counter drinking coffee.

"Morning, Mom, Dad."

"Good morning, Savannah. You're up early." Her mother smiled.

"I know. I just received a phone call… A case I'm working on has gotten … dangerous. They're going to start driving by the house and keeping an eye out. I'd like you to be wary of any suspicious-looking people, cars, et cetera. "

"What's going on?" Her mother frowned.

"I'm not at liberty to say. This is more of a precautionary measure than anything else."

"We'll keep our eyes peeled. You stay safe out there." Her Father always knew how to smooth ruffled feathers when it came to Mom.

"I will. I'm going to go get dressed. I need to be in the office."She turned and headed for the stairs.

"What about breakfast?" Her mother called after her.

"I'll grab bagels on the way out, I promise."

A quick shower later and she was dressed in a pair of khaki pants, a light pink shirt, and a pair of brown boots. Her hair was slicked back from her face. She'd applied a light coat of make-up to hide her sleep-weary face. With her badge tucked into her belt and her gun on her hip, concealed by a blazer, she stomped down the stairs and rushed into the kitchen.

"See, Mom, I'm getting breakfast like I promised." She cut a bagel in two, slathered it with strawberry cream cheese from the fridge, and poured a glass of orange juice into her travel cup.

"Mmhmm." Her mother quirked an eyebrow but continued eating.

"I'll see you guys later. Call me if you need anything." She exchanged a meaningful look with her father. He'd be on the lookout for anything out of the normal, and his gun was in a safe by the bed. He wouldn't hesitate to use it, if need be. The knowledge filled her with a sense of relief. He might be retired, but her father was still sharp as a tack, and a crack shot.

He kept up a relaxed, but steady workout regime accompanied with a biweekly trip to the shooting range. She knew her Mother was worried, though she'd never admit it. It was a part of having family members in a dangerous profession. You put on a good front to keep the worry from them so they could act with a clear mind. It took a toll. It was the price paid by those who loved someone with a calling to protect and serve.

She hooked the travel mug onto her satchel and took a bite of the round circle of bread. After snatching her keys from the counter, she exited the house. Ten minutes later she was in front of the police station finishing off her cup of orange juice. With one last gulp she grabbed her mug and exited the car. Long strides took her inside the building. Time seemed to slow as she waved to the receptionist and walked to the office she shared with Carey.

Everyone's gaze followed her. This case had been the one that got away. They were all eager to solve it and avenge one of their own. She opened the door to her office. Carey sat at his desk, doing his best not to stare at the small, manila envelope.

"Thank God! I've been itching to open this thing all morning!" He pushed his chair back and swiveled to face her.

"What happened with that exactly?"

"They brought in the dogs to test if for explosives or hazardous items. It came out clean."

"So I have the go-ahead?"

"Yep."

"Good, let's go get suited up."

"Music to my ears!"

She laughed as she placed her bag onto the desk and removed a set of gloves to handle the package with.

After all the anticipation, the tiny, fur-covered object Vannah pulled from its yellow prison was anti-climatic. He wrinkled his brow.

"What the hell is that?" he asked with a snort. Greeted with quiet, he turned to look down at Vannah and his heart sank. Something was very wrong. The tongs shook where she held the tiny, brown, plush bear holding a heart. Her breathing was ragged, and her eyes were wide with dilated pupils.

"Vannah?"

"I won this for him … at the carnival." Her voice was empty and monotone.

Fuck. She seemed glued to the spot, unable to move, as she clenched the tongs hard enough to turn her knuckles white. Her eyes glazed over, and he knew her mind was no longer in the present. *Every time she turns around she's forced to relive bit and pieces of her ordeal. But somehow to have an actual bit of history from that night was the cruelest twist the wheel of fate had delivered.*

She took a deep breath, and her face crumpled like a wadded piece of paper. He wanted to look away, pretend he hadn't seen the wounded woman beneath the hardnosed agent persona she embodied. Yet, he promised Clark. Old habits died hard.

He placed his hands over hers, helping her lower the bear to the counter before he removed the tongs from her hand. Chest heaving and shoulders shaking, she balled her fists and bowed her head.

"It's okay, Vannah." He wrapped an arm around her shoulders and pulled her into his body. He could hear the hiccups she swallowed and knew she was tittering on the edge of a meltdown.

"Shh." He placed a gentle kiss on the top of her head. "Let's take a break."

Leading her to the stools across the room, he helped her sit. She clenched her jaw. Seeing the silent fight to contain her anguish made him feel like a voyeur. Words escaped him. Everything that popped into his head sounded too contrived or ignorant. So he held his tongue, rubbed her back, and waited for a cue. A few minutes later she cleared her throat.

"I'm okay." Her back stiffened. She pulled away from his hand.

"No."

"What?"

He refused to let the curt tone put him off. "After all of that there's no way I'm going to step back and pretend it never happened."

"Why? It'd work for me," she mumbled.

"Because you have to talk about this."

"I really don't." She shook her head.

"Vannah, have you ever thought your refusal to deal with this head-on might be affecting Clark?"

"What are you talking about?" Her eyes flashed with anger.

"You know what keeps a spirit earthbound? Unfinished business."

"I'm not going to sit here and listen to this." She removed her gloves with loud snaps and spun around, ready to leave. He placed a hand on her shoulder, stopping her retreat.

"Yes, you will. He knows you aren't the same. Do you think it doesn't affect him?"

"That's his choice." The words were unconvincing.

"Bullshit."

She sighed. "What do you want me to do, Carey?"

"I want you to stop acting like a damn robot, and feel," he growled, frustrated by her lack of empathy.

"You have no clue what I'm like outside of work." Her lips curled upward in a sneer.

"No, but I bet Clark does."

"He told you about last night, didn't he?" She glanced up, releasing a deep breath that tossled the wayward tufts of hair framing her face.

They never kept secrets from one another. Why should now be any different?

"He mentioned it, yeah. What were you thinking, leading him on like that?"

"Leading him on? I was honest about my feelings. I felt he deserved to know." She placed her hands on her knees and leaned forward.

"Why? Nothing could come of it."

"He's not the only one who's suffered from the need for closure all this time, Carey!" She rocked back, stretched to her full seated height, and glared.

"Aha! So you admit it." He pointed to her, pleased that he'd gotten her to respond.

"Son of a bitch!" She threw her hands up in the air and rose from the stool. "You did that on purpose, didn't you? Sneaky bastard!" The narrowed stare she pinned him with made him antsy.

"I don't think Mom would appreciate that."

"This isn't a game."

He sobered. "No, it's not. I'm sorry. I was just trying to lighten the moment. This whole situation is so heavy. I feel like I'm caught up in a rockslide on a daily basis. You have to let go, Vannah.

Turning your life into some sort of living shrine to Clark isn't good for either of you."

"I'm not." She shook her head vehemently.

"Aren't you? When's the last time you went on a date, held a steady relationship?"

"What's wrong with putting your career first?" Arms crossed over her chest, she leaned her weight back onto one leg.

"Nothing, but for you it's all that exists."

"I do other things," she mumbled.

"Name three for me." He arched his eyebrow.

She paused. "Travel."

"Is it for work?"

"Not always."

"Okay, I'll give you that. Two more." He held up two fingers.

"Read."

"Uh huh." His voice dripped with disbelief as he gestured for her to follow with a wave of his hand. "Next."

"I do things with my best friend Amy."

"And that fulfills you?"

"Not everyone wants a husband and kids, Carey."

"No, but you always did."

She placed her tongue in her cheek and breathed through her nostrils, tilting her head back. "After what happened I saw life differently. Around every corner there was pain, evil, and devastation. I wanted to be a light, someone who answered the questions that kept people up at night and combated the wrongdoings. The ideal of bringing a new life into a world full of so much bad terrifies me. Let alone giving my heart to someone else. That kind of commitment opens you up to a hurt that cuts you to the core. Leave scars that change you indefinitely. I don't want to go through that again."

"You're missing out on so much because you're afraid of what-ifs."

"Maybe." She pierced him with her determined gaze. "But it's my choice."

"Even if it keeps Clark here?"

Her shoulders slumped. "You really think that's why they sent him back?"

"I think it's a huge part of it. Coupled with the way he died."

She rubbed her temples with her fingertips. "What do I do?"

"You have to show him the old you is still inside there somewhere, and you're happy."

"Happy's relative." Her quick retort rang false.

"Not to Clark… not to me."

"Why the sudden change of heart?" In full detective mode she studied him, like Sherlock Holmes on a case.

"Now that I finally have you here in Dale, I'm doing what I should've done a long time ago." He might be doing this for Clark, but he meant what he said. His brother just gave him a nudge in the right direction to get the ball rolling.

"Which is what?" Her face twisted into a bitter sneer. "Hold my hand while I cry? Tell me it's going to be all right, and I should move on?"

"No." He shook his head. "I'm going to drag you back to life, kicking and screaming if I have to."

"I'd like to see you try."

"Is that a challenge?" He tilted his head to the side.

"That's a fuck you, Carey Carr."

"I expected as much. Doesn't change my position."

"I'm not a case to be solved."

"I didn't say that." He paused. "Do you trust me?"

"Obviously. We're working together."

"Then please allow me to help you let go."

"And you made your peace?"

"Yes. I'll always miss Clark. The hole he left will never be filled. Every year when his disappearance rolls around I'll get a little wasted. I was lost for a long while. Eventually I realized life had to keep moving forward. He would've wanted me to be happy."

"Are you?"

"I think so. I mean… there are things I don't have and I'd like to, but isn't that the story of everyone's life?"

"How'd you do it?" Her face softened. Emotion bled through her voice.

"It just came with time. I was here in town living with the stares and the whispers. Packaging it up in the back of my mind in a neat little compartment wasn't an option. So I worked through the volatile emotions, self-loathing, guilt, pity. You know all the usual suspects in a situation like this."

"For the record, I have no issues with the way I am. I'm happy. But I refuse to be the reason Clark is stuck with one foot in Heaven and the other on earth."

"Thank you." Mentally he breathed a sigh of relief.

"I need to go and call this in to the Bureau."

"You think they'll come in with guns blazing?"

"This crime was committed in Dale. So it's a local issue. Unless we get proof of more victims in other places, they don't really have a reason to."

"Good." He held up a hand. "No offense."

She snorted. "None taken."

"Are you ready to get back to work, or do you want to leave the room for a bit?"

"No, I'm good now. Thank you."

Carey nodded. She walked back over to the examination table, placing on a new pair of gloves. He moved over to stand at her side. "Do you think you'll find something?"

"Chances are they're trying to bait me. Make me aware of their presence."

In the end nothing she could see yielded any clues. She was forced to admit defeat and pass the bear on to the lab.

"Come on, Vannah. Let's go get lunch somewhere."

"I'm not feeling social."

"We'll eat at my place. You need to get out of here for awhile. Shake it off, get some fuel in your belly, and come back fresh."

"Maybe you're right."

"I am." He walked over to her chair and held out his hand. She grabbed it, and a shock of awareness ran through him. "Come on." She allowed him to pull her up. Her graceful hand fit his like a glove. The realization stunned.

He scanned the area. Was Clark nearby? The rumor about twins sharing thoughts, and emotions was true. Even after Clark passed, he could sense him. At first he thought he'd been headed for the psych ward. Then he'd done some research and found it wasn't uncommon.

She dropped his hand and they walked through the door. *Maybe lunch at my place wasn't the best idea.* The mood was subdued and they didn't say much as they left the station.

"I'll drive," he offered.

"Okay."

Her lackluster response made him frown. "We're doing all we can, Vannah." He unlocked the car with his key fob.

"I know, but it doesn't seem like enough." She opened the door and entered the car, shutting the door before he could respond. *I can take a hint, no conversation.* He got into the driver's seat, turned on the radio. After starting the engine, he pulled out of the parking lot.

Ten minutes later they were inside his kitchen. She sat at the four-person, square oak table. He stood in front of the fridge.

"What are you in the mood for? I have cold cuts, steak, pasta?" He turned to look over his shoulder.

"Whatever you're in the mood for."

Get her minds off things. "Okay, banana pancakes it is."

"What?" she chuckled half-heartedly.

I'll take it. "That's better. Steak and a salad okay?"

"It's great, but salad?" Wrinkling her nose, she frowned.

68

"Hey, gotta watch my figure."

"Really?"

He laughed. "Okay, have to make sure I'm faster than the perpetrators I'm pursuing."

"Better, but in Dale?" Her eyes laughed at him.

"Careful, your big city snobbery is showing."

She rolled her eyes. "Please, I know where I come from."

"Hmph." He pulled out the steak, opened the packaging, and began to season.

"Are you saying I don't?" Fire returned in her voice. *Mission accomplished.*

"I'm just curious. Do you even remember how to play Farkle?" They'd spent hours playing the dice game when they were younger.

"Yes, and I bet I can still mop the floor with you."

He smirked. *Got you!* "In your dreams, sweetheart."

"Once lunch is over we'll see."

"I guess so."

Soon the meat was cooked, the salad was prepared and on the table.

"Wow, Carey. I'm impressed with your domestic abilities."

"Yeah unlike Peter Pan, I eventually had to grow up."

"I would've liked to see that." The wistful tone of her voice made him reach over and place his hands over hers. "No more what-if's, Vannah. We can't go back and change the past."

"You're right." She nodded.

"Good. I'm going to remind you of this moment the next time you're pissed at me."

She chuckled. "I forgot how funny you were."

"That's because you've been away too long, and I have to admit I got better with time."

"I love your modesty."

"It's one of my more charming attributes." He took his seat

69

across from her and set their plates on the table. "Let's eat. I'm suddenly in the mood for Farkle."

They dug into their food. He kept the conversation light and humorous. The taut muscles in his shoulders relaxed.

"I'll help you clean up." She stood, cleared the table, and he followed. The banter proved easy to slip back into. He watched her from the corner of his eye as they rinsed their plates and utensils and placed them in the dishwasher.

Relaxed and bemused, she glowed. He could see the women she would have been if Clark's murder had never happened.

"Why are your eyes boring a hole into me?"

"Just enjoying the moment."

"Uh huh?" She closed the door to the dishwasher and stood." Don't try to get out of Farkle. I'm ready to crush you."

"Jeez, you're all heart. I'll grab the dice. You do remember the rules, right?"

"Yes, you smarmy bastard."

She moved back to the table as he opened a drawer beside the sink, chuckling. Vannah always gave as good as she got. They managed to trash talk their way through three games before they packed up. She'd made good on her boast, earning the high score.

"This was more fun than I thought it'd be."

"Good?"

"Yeah."

"So you wouldn't be opposed to doing it again?"

"No, I wouldn't." The smile faded from her lip, and her expression grew serious. "But now it's time to get back to work."

"Yeah."

It was interesting the way she hid behind her job. He left off the serious discussions for later. He had to go slow, or she'd balk. There was too much at stake now for him to fail. When this was all finished Clark needed to go home where he belonged. The thought hurt. The selfish part of him loved having Clark here in a physical sense, but what happened when they all died and he remained alone with no one to talk to? He'd seen enough paranormal movies to know spirits that hung on too long went south. *I'll be damned if I'll let that happen to Clark.*

Chapter Six

Is this compete with Savannah month?" she asked, only partially joking. Last week they'd started the tradition of playing Farkle during their lunch breaks. This week he wanted to go play Putt-putt. She'd held her breath in anticipation of the touchy-feely stuff to come. Per his style.

He'd done the exact opposite of what was expected and kept things on a laidback level she could easily handle. Between worrying about her family, looking around every corner for Clark, and pulling late nights, her brain was close to mush.

"No, I just thought it'd be fun to check out all the old haunts, sort of past meets present take on things. I figured maybe it'd help us find our new normal." He shrugged. The slight tint to his cheeks told her this was hard for him. So she bit back the smart -leck comments that rolled into her head. *This is for Clark, and I've been bitchy enough to Carey to last a lifetime.*

"When do you want to go?"

"Tonight. I mean it is a Friday and I'd rather not seem like a loser with no life."

His words made her cringe. The days had begun to blur together. Without Amy to drag her out to do non-work related things she'd gone into workaholic mode.

"Seven okay?" he asked.

"Perfect. Are we eating there?"

"Of course, how could I pass up the best hot dogs in the county?" His face twisted into an expression of mock-offense and she laughed.

"I was always partial to the nachos myself."

"I remember." His voice turned solemn.

She smiled as memories flooded back. The three of them had whiled away many nights at the Hole in One growing up. It was a rite of passage being able to go there parentless. When she'd shut the vault door on her time growing up in Dale, she'd lost a lot of the good things as well. Her chest tightened and he pushed the sullen thoughts into the back of her mind. They wouldn't help her or Clark.

"I guess I'll see you there then?"

"Definitely."

They headed in opposite directions from the entryway, and she got into her SUV. She pulled out of the parking lot. Clark appeared. She jumped, swerved, and regained control.

"Jesus, Clark, are you trying to kill me?" Her heart raced and she placed a hand on her chest as she caught her breath.

"No, sorry, I thought now would be a good time to chat."

"Next time show up before the car is in motion, okay?"

"Okay." The gentle, subdued tone stole her ire.

She shook he head. *I've never been able to stay mad at him.* "You haven't been around lately."

"I needed time to process."

"Boy, can I relate to that."

"I'm not sorry I told you how I felt. I spent years in anguish over that. I am sorry for storming off like a sulky child. I knew this wasn't going to be easy." The contemplative tone seemed more for him than her. "Still, the reality differed vastly from the way I envisioned it in my head."

"It always does. I should apologize for leading you on. I got caught up in the moment and the excitement of knowing you felt the same way. That night at the carnival I planned on telling you how I felt. Not getting that opportunity gutted me." She risked a glance out of her peripheral in his direction. The reverent expression on his face brought pain, and comfort. For so long she'd wondered if her love had been unrequited, or the figment of a very young and active imagination. "We both know this can't go anywhere."

"I know." A rueful smile tipped up the corner of his mouth. "Doesn't mean I don't wish it could though."

She placed a hand over his. "Me too." She squeezed and released his hand, returning hers to the shifter. "Are we good now?"

"I think so." The low hum of wheels on the road filled the car. "How's the case coming?"

"Slower than I'd like." She huffed. Cases never fell into your lap the way they did on television. It took a lot of work and digging. Usually by now she'd have something solid. Flying blind didn't sit well with her.

"They want to make a grand entrance," he scoffed.

"Do you know that for sure?" Images of random acts of violence filled her head: fires, bombings, and personal attacks on innocent people. Her throat clogged and her chest ached.

"I sense it. But I have no more knowledge than you."

"They sent you down here without any intel?" *It didn't make any sense.*

"Isn't that what faith is all about? Trusting in things unseen?"

"Someone was paying attention during Religion class."

"I've had a lot of time to ponder."

His wry comment brought home the fact that he was a ghost. It was too easy to lose herself in the vivid illusion.

"What made you become an F.B.I agent, Vannah? That's light years away from a grade school teacher."

"You don't know?" *Hadn't he been watching over them?*

"I could only observe, and even then, not all the time. Think of it as watching movie previews. It wasn't creepy in the way people

75

make it seem in the movies. We don't just hang around and follow you from room to room, watching you sleep."

"Would you hate me if I said that was good to know?" She cringed.

He laughed. "No. You're the same girl who thought Santa was a pervert for knowing when you were sleeping and awake. Because it led to the question, 'Is he spying on you when you were in the shower and getting dressed'."

"What? It was a valid question." She took a right on Fifth and headed toward Main Street, passing their old middle school.

Clark snorted but held his peace.

"I guess it was my response to what happened. I needed to do something that would make a difference for other victims like me. I thought of going into counseling at first. It's what led me to my psychology classes. In the end it didn't seem hand- on enough. Plus, I felt like I'd be lying." The trip down memory lane made her shift in her seat.

"Lying to whom?"

"The children I'd teach. Telling them the world was a safe place to venture out into when I knew different. Their wide-eyed innocence would have filleted me alive back then."

"And now?"

Time to lay all the cards on the table. "Now I envy it."

"You know it wasn't your fault I didn't escape."

Air left her lungs in a whoosh. She pulled over a few yards from her house. Clenching her eyes shut, she rode out the tsunami of emotions. Pain, anger, relief, and guilt, pounded against her like ruthless rain. Gripping the wheel, blood rushed in her ears and her head grew light. She felt disconnected from her physical body. *Could he see through to all the quiet thoughts and concerns she held close?*

"H-how did you know?"

"Because I know you, Savannah West. You take everything on to yourself and find letting go damn near impossible. You'd bring up silly mistakes you'd made years ago growing up. How could you not do the same thing with this? I knew what I was risking when I used the momentum of my body to force you out of the trunk. I wouldn't change it if I'd known how things would turn out. That was when my life was supposed to end."

"Clark." Her voice cracked.

"No, you need to hear this, Savannah. I love you. There is no greater gift than to lay down your life for a friend. You are my female counterpart to Carey. Without you things would never be right. Personally, I don't think I'd have your strength. You dealt with this situation with dignity, and a quiet grace I never could've pulled off. That's always been you though. You possess this superhuman ability to shoulder the weight of the world and still keep moving forward. It's one of the things I love most about you."

She swiped at the tears that obscured her vision. "Y-yes you could." She turned her head to find his face wet with his sorrow-filled drops of saline. He leaned in and rested his forehead against hers. "You and Carey have to take care of each other now, Savannah. I couldn't bear it if they got a hold of either of you. If I can set things right, I'll walk away happy."

"How can it ever be set right?" *No matter what we accomplish here Clark will still leave.*

"It's already starting."

"W-what do you mean?" Their whispered voices filled the quiet space. Time seemed to exist in a bubble.

"You and Carey reconciling."

She narrowed her eyes. "Why is that so important to you?"

"Because having the two people I love most in the world at odds was killing me. He makes you laugh… and remember. I always felt like when you left here you put me in a tidy box, swept under you bed, and only pulled out when my anniversary came back. I didn't want to be that."

"Clark, I think about you all the time." Pulling away, she shook her head.

"Yes, but never the happy times. It's always overshadowed by my death. I don't want to be the cause of so much pain, not anymore." He brought his hands up to stroke her hair. "No more hurting yourself on my account, Vannah, please."

"I'm sorry." Her body shook. "I had no idea—"

"I know. But now that you do I need a promise. You never renege on those."

"What do you want me to promise?" *I don't like this.*

"That you will battle your way to the place and time when thoughts of me make you smile, and add happiness and joy." He delivered a shaky smile.

"Clark –"

"I know you don't think you can do it, but you can. I have faith in you. The strength you possess is so much greater than you've ever realized. Hell, I think it kept me fed a time or two when I was at my lowest." His hands stilled and he leaned back in, pressed his lips to hers. The kiss tasted like goodbye. "We can't do this to ourselves anymore, Savannah. It's time to let go of the missed opportunity."

"Are you leaving?" Panic tensed her muscles. *I'm not ready!*

"Not until this is done. But I won't make so free with you. It's not right." The words sliced through her, deflated the tiny balloon of hope that had begun to rise. He placed a finger on her lips. "It's a lot to take in right now, I know. I think we both need space." She wanted to grab onto him and beg him to stay. The open dialogue was freeing.

With him at her side, the gaping pit of pain, guilt, and a lifetime of memories felt surmountable. "Remember you promised, Vannah. No shutting down or going back to the way it was before. Lean on, Carey. He's ready to be your rock." He moved back. Covering her mouth with her hand she muffled the cry of protest that burst free when he disappeared.

I can't go inside like this. A look in her rearview mirror told her she was a red-rimmed, puffy-nosed mess. A few cleansing breaths later she pulled out into traffic and headed toward the one person she knew would understand–Carey.

A knock came at the door. Carey frowned. He grabbed his gun from its holster. Took off the safety and walked toward the door. Though he'd never voiced his concern out loud he realized through him the killers had a second chance to complete their crime without the hang-ups. His steps were carefully measured and silent on the carpeted floor. With his back against the wall he leaned over and peered out the peephole.

The sight of Vannah worried and relieved him at the same time. He clicked the safety back into place, lowered the gun, and opened the door.

"What happened, Vannah?"

She stepped inside and wrapped her arms around her waist. He rubbed her arms.

"I saw Clark, and after that I-I couldn't go home like this." She gestured toward her swollen face with her hands. "They'd ask questions I couldn't answer."

"Are you okay? Is he?"

"No." Her lower lip trembled. "Yes."

"No, you aren't okay or..." Carey shrugged, trying to read her. This was such a far departure from the woman he'd come to know. *I have no clue how to approach her without getting my head bit off.*

"I don't even know what I am."

"Okay." He paused. "Why don't we move to the couch and you can start at the beginning." He placed a hand on the small of her back. Shut and locked the door and guided her to the couch.

"He showed up in the car. We talked about what happened the other night, made our peace. And he said... we couldn't go there anymore." Her words were skewed. barely discernible as she re-laid the story, pausing frequently to hold it together.

"I don't." He scratched the back of his neck. "Um. I'm not sure what to say to all that."

"I wasn't expecting you to say anything really. I just needed to tell someone. I know it had to happen. But I wasn't ready. I never would have been. How do you prepare to have your heart ripped out? Being back here makes everything seem fresh."

"Is that really such a bad thing?" Carey whispered.

"Not anymore." She sniffed.

"That's good then… right?" He arched an eyebrow and she gave a shaky laugh.

"Yes."

"So… no Hole in One?"

She threw her head back and laughed. A husky chuckle that made him re-distribute his weight on the couch. *Now is not the time.*

"No, I think we should, though I'm not dressed for it at all."

"You're fine, but you might want to … wash your face." He circled his face with his hand.

"God! I probably look a fright." She placed palms on her cheeks and stood. "I'll go clean up. I'm a little dressy for Hole in One, but it'll do."

He couldn't help but admire the high, firm ass highlighted by her black slacks when she walked off. Forcing his gaze up to the ceiling he counted to ten. *Think cold shower, and calm oceans. If she comes back and sees I have a har- on she's going to think I'm a total scum bag. Should've cleaned the pipes.*

By the time she came back he had *things* under control.

"I'm ready."

"Good, let's go." *Before I embarrass myself.*

Chapter Seven

Savannah pressed the cold glass of iced tea to her neck. It was a sweltering summer, and her parents' air conditioner was on the fritz. Which chased her over to Carey's while they worked on their case after hours. *I wonder if Clark has something to do with that.* The case had become an all-consuming driving force for both of them.

Frustrated by their inability to move forward they'd opted to take a break.

"When are your parents going to get the air fixed... not that I mind." His gaze raked over her. "I like the view."

"Flirt. I just spent the drive over here sweating like a pig. I doubt I'm much to look at."

"Don't underestimate your appeal." The gravelly quality of his voice touched her in places long unattended. Clearing her throat, she attempted to refocus her attention on anything other than the sexy man who sat across from her in a white tank top and a pair of sweats. No matter how hard she tried, she couldn't keep her gaze from his tats.

"Okay, I have to ask. What do the tattoos mean?"

"Aaah. The million dollar question."

"Is it a secret?" Intrigued, she sat up straight.

"No, just personal." Red appeared in his cheeks. "It's a memorial."

"That makes perfect sense. Why are you embarrassed?" She arched an eyebrow.

"It's for the three of us… I sort of felt like we died with Clark." He placed his hand on his arm. "The rose in the Rosary represents you."

"I'm on your arm?" she whispered. Touched, she covered her mouth.

"I couldn't do the piece without you. It didn't feel right. When I first started work on this I knew I wanted us all on a rosary, connected despite everything that went down."

"Carey." Unable to find the right words, she shook her head.

"See, this is why I didn't want to talk about it." He rubbed the back of his neck.

"What have you been telling people all this time?"

"That it's a memorial tat for my twin brother. They don't ask for more detail after that."

"Am I the only one who knows?"

"Yeah." His jaw was tensed. He refused to meet her gaze. Setting her drink on the table, she walked over to him and sank onto the arm of his chair. She traced the rosary that faded into the background of the brightly-colored, old school sailor designs that surrounded it. There were red stars, a red and blue swallow, and a set of dice.

"Thank you," she whispered.

He tilted his head up. Their gazes locked.

"Want to hear something funny?"

"Sure." He nodded, his voice equally soft.

Stepping back, she pulled up the hem of her tank top and lowered the top of her cutoff shorts. A delicate brown branch with three blossoms, black, red, and pink, graced the curve of her hip.

"For us?"

She nodded. A slow smile erased the pinched, austere expression he'd held moments earlier. He extended a finger and traced over the pattern. She sucked in a breath. A searing heat spread through her body. Her pulse kicked into overdrive and her muscles tensed. His finger crept lower, brushing the top of her shorts. Holding her breath in anticipation of more, she watched him through half closed lids.

"Savannah?" Raspy and uncertain, his question asked for permission.

"Y-yes." The words were out before she could overthink them. His head dipped and his tongue shot out and caressed the path his digit had traced.

"Oh." Her nipples hardened and her pussy grew moist. Years of neglect combined together to overthrow her objections. Desire exploded inside her like a bomb, superseding her common sense. Latching her fingers onto his shoulde,r she allowed her head to fall back, enjoying the feel of his mouth. He nipped her skin, moving across her waist. The stubble on his chin tickled where it grazed her delicate skin. He paused at her belly button and dipped his tongue inside. Her stomach muscles quivered, and her toes curled in her flip-flops. He pulled back, blowing on her wet skin.

"Carey."The wobbly words made him look up.

"Do you want me to stop, Vannah?"

"N-no."

Holding her stare, he brought his hand up and cupped her pussy. She gasped.

"Still okay?"

Unable to speak, she nodded. He began a massage.

"Oooh." In need of relief from the pounding rhythm of need emitting from her core she spread her legs to allow him more room to play.

"That's it, baby, open up for me." Her legs trembled. The rough material pressed into her cleft. She rocked her hips against him. Needy mewls slipped from her mouth.

"It feels so good," she moaned.

"Are you going to come for me, Vannah/"

"Y-yes."

"Mmm. I can feel the heat from your pussy through your shorts. Are you going to let me taste you after I make you come?"

The erotic image of his head between her legs sent her hurtling up the precipice she'd climbed to at the speed of light.

The sound of a zipper being pulled down brought her back to the present. He parted the miniscule piece of fabric and worked it down her hip, stopping to kiss the new patch of skin revealed to his hungry gaze. Shoving the shorts to her ankles, he hovered in front of her moist center.

"I can smell how badly you want me, Vannah." He ran his fingers along the side of her boy-cut black briefs, and she trembled. His finger slipped inside and caressed her swollen clit. She purred.

"I like that sound. I want to hear you make it again." He circled her swollen nub a few more times and dipped into her entrance. "You're so hot and tight."

"Carey." Whimpering, she begged him for release with her eyes.

"I always was a sucker for those eyes." Removing his hand, he slipped his fingers into his mouth and moaned. "You're delicious. I think I need a better taste."

He pushed down her underwear and latched his mouth onto her pussy in one swift swoop.

"Oh God!"

Sucking her clit into his mouth, he hummed, inserting a finger, and began to thrust. She buried her fingers into his soft hair and writhed. The pressure began to build. Her walls quivered. He pulled away.

"No!"

"I want to be inside you when you come. Buried so deep neither of us can remember all the fucked-up shit going on around us."

The raw honesty behind his words killed herfaster than any prettied words would have.

"Yes."

"Thank God." His mumbled words made her smirk. Kicking off her flip flops, she stepped from the material encasing her ankles.

He stood, shoving his sweatpants and boxers down around his ankles as he sat back down on the chair. His cock sprang free. Ten inches of quivering male seeped milky white fluid. A vein ran on the underside of his girth. There would be no bed, dim lighting, or whispers. This was release and comfort. A moment of blissful peace during the constant barrage of pain they'd been forced into at every turn with this case.

"Protection?"

Swiveling his chair he rummaged in the desk drawer and turned back around with a reflective square in his hand. She snatched it from his fingertips and grinned.

"I believe it's my turn."

With a firm grip on his cock she bent and flicked the vein that stood out in his swollen member. He jerked and grunted. The guttural sound made her pussy gush liquid that spilled onto her upper thighs.

"Vannah." Pulling back, she stroked him until iridescent beads of liquid flowed in a steady stream. Licking her hand clean she opened the square and rolled the condom down on his rock-hard shaft. She climbed onto his lap.

"Guide yourself in, Carey."

When he grasped the base of his cock, she eased down onto him. Her fingers dug into his shoulders as he spread her walls. Flexing around him, she moaned. His masculine grunt joined her as she stretched to accommodate him inch by inch.

When she was fully seated she nodded. He grasped her hips, lifted her up, and brought her down in smooth strokes that made her cry out. Their gazes were like lasers locked onto a target. There were no words. The sound of lovemaking and rapid breathing filled the room.

Her muscles clamped down on him. A miniature earthquake swept through her body. White light flooded behind her eyelids. Pumping faster, he rode through the explosion, joining her a few moments later. His harsh, strangled cry echoed in her ears.

Spent, she draped herself over him. Their sweat-slickened bodies molded together as they came down.

"Wow seems like an underwhelming word, but it's all I got."

She laughed and he breathed a mental sigh of relief. *We're going to be okay.*

"No, I'd say that about sums it up."

"Good." Brushing a stray strand of hair behind her ear, he offered up a genuine smile. "Thank you, Savannah."

"You're welcome." They leaned in as one, lips connecting, and throwing sparks very different from the ones that had led them into this position.

"Thank you." The words whispered against his lips did funny things to his stomach. Girly things he didn't dare thinkg too hard on. Alarm bells rang and red flags waved. *I can't afford to do this. She's my partner. Right now this case is all that matters. Oh God… Clark.* His ardor quickly became cooled. *How am I going to explain this? I just did the one thing he'll never be able to.* Guilt rushed in like a flash flood, clogging his throat and making it hard to breathe.

"We should get cleaned up, huh?" He feigned normalcy, hoping she wouldn't pick up on his unease.

"Yeah. I have to say this wasn't the cool-down method I had in mind when I came over." Her wry delivery made him snort.

"No? And here I thought you'd been planning this for weeks."

"Oh, you got me, Carey." Her high-pitched mockery moved them into more familiar territory. She drew back and stood. "I'm going to shower in the guest room." He nodded. "Meet you out here in fifteen?"

"Sounds good."

Despite the nudity they'd slipped back into their partner roles. They both knew this case was too big to blow over feelings, sexual or other. *Jesus, when I dig a hole, I dig it deep.* Lost in his musings, he disposed the condom in the master bathroom.

The hot shower rinsed away the dirt and majority of the guilt. Dry, he redressed in a light blue polo and a pair of khaki cargo shorts. Barefoot and refreshed, he turned to head for the door and came up short. Clark stood in front of the door, an odd expression on his face. *He knows!*

"I wanted this to happen. At least... I thought I did. But I never imagined it'd be this fast." His voice was thoughtful. He glanced up, his eyes unnaturally bright with pain and anger. It sent a shiver skittering down Carey's spine.

"Clark... it's not ... we're not in a relationship." At a loss for word,s Carey shook his head.

"Yet... but you will be."

Carey's attempt to placate was batted away like a cat with a ball of yarn. "That's a lot of assumptions."

"Can you honestly tell me you aren't looking at her now wondering what-if?" Clark growled.

"Wondering and doing are two different things, and you know it."

"Mmhmm. I'm not the only one in this room who thinks that sounds lame."

"What were you just sitting around watching us?" Stunned by the words he let fly, Carey turned his head. A part of him still waited for the other shoe to drop with Clark. What was the downside to returning? It felt too good to be true.

"Not that I have anything better to do, but no. I popped in with an update. Perhaps I should've phoned, or at least knocked."

Carey sighed. "I'm sorry, Clark. I honestly didn't have this planned. It just sort of... happened."

"That's what they all say."

The knife in his heart turned a bit deeper.

"Clark."

"I'm just giving you shit. Better you than anyone else. I got a tip." He shrugged but sadness clung to him. "A tip."

"An insight on the killers. I heard it through the grapevine. The tarot card obsession is strange, and where I live folks have a long memory."

"Grapevine?" Carey shook his head.

"Spirits talk, they hear things you know? I think I pinpointed the men we're talking about. I don't have a name but I do have descriptions and a possible hometown location."

"Are you serious?"

The stern look he gave spoke volumes.

"Of course you are. Let's go out front and meet up with Vannah. I'll take notes."

"Fantastic. Then the Scooby gang can be together again."

"If you want her to move on, don't you think you should take the same advice?" He left the room before Clark could answer. *Let him chew on that for a while.*

Vannah was seated on the couch, flipping through television stations, when he entered.

"We got company. Clark stopped by with some info on the killers."

Her eyes widened and her jaw dropped.

"Does he know?" she mouthed.

"Yeah, he figured it out."

She winced, and he nodded.

Footfalls sounded on the floor behind him. He turned. Held his breath as he waited for Clark to speak.

"Hey, Vannah." Hands shoved in his pocket, and his shoulders hunched, Clark looked defeated.

"Hey, Clark, what's up?" Pain flickered in the depths of her dark eyes. *We went from the three musketeers to the walking wounded.*

"I think I might have a description and stomping grounds. The tarot card fetish is a dead giveaway. It's two Caucasian males mid-forties to mid-fifties. They have dark hair they tend to keep mid-length and dark eyes. They're tall, over six feet and lanky. I don't know if it'll help. But I figured it was more than you had now." He shrugged.

"How do you know all that?" Vannah narrowed her eyes.

"Ghost hotline."

"Wow, thank you, Clark." She shifted on the couch, and Carey could see her discomfort. If it was because they'd been caught in the act or she'd been reminded he was a ghost, he couldn't say. The whole ghost tip made him uneasy.

"I'm just glad to finally be of some use. It's been pretty anti-climatic. I come down and do what? Pop in and out."

"I think Carey and I both agree just seeing you changed our lives irrevocably. You can't be more poignant than that."

"Well, when you say it that way." Clark smiled.

For a brief moment it was like time had reversed and they were as they had always been. Carey savored the moment, held it close to his heart. Clark's return had been an upheaval, unearthing emotions, and unresolved issues that had been ignored for years. This was the good part, a new happy memory to get him through the darkness creeping in around them.

Chapter Eight

Damnit!" Savannah slapped her palms against the desk. Frustrated, she shoved away from the wooden prison she'd been chained too for what felt like an eternity. *A week of searching, and nothing!*

"It's like these guys are ghosts! I can't find hide nor hair of them. No loose ends, no cases that line up or bodies that fit the description. If they did all these kills based on cards, where are the remains?" Not expecting an answer, she paced the tiny confines of the office.

"Listen, it's getting late. Why don't we call it?" Carey's reasonable suggestion made her surly. *I'm like a lion with a thorn in its paw.* She wanted to snarl and hurl a cutting comment. Instead she walked over to the window and peered out. The sun had begun to fall from the sky lighting the sun up all golden and pink. Right now the people of Dale were out enjoying the beauty, blissfully unaware of the sick bastards who moved among them in the shadows. It gutted her.

She ran a hand through her hair and nodded. Her nerves were paper thin. The walls around them seemed to shrink. The need to escape hit her like a roundhouse to the chest. On autopilot she returned to her laptop and shut it down.

"You don't look right."

"I don't feel it either. Burning the wick from both ends and I'm ready to just … "

"Run away?"

"Yeah." Pressing her middle finger and her thumb into her temples, she issued a light massage.

"Let's go then."

"What?" She shook her head. "A weekend camped out in your apartment wasn't what I had in mind."

"Me either but don't act like you wouldn't love every second."

"Hmm." Her body hummed with the unspoken promise his words held. Stress release sounded right up her alley.

"Save it." The knowing look in his eyes intrigued her.

"For?" Confused she furrowed her brow.

"The lake house."

The quaint log cabin nestled in the woods an hour away flashed in her mind.

"No."

"Come on, we always had fun up there."

"That's the problem." Her muttered words were low. His narrowed eyes told her he'd heard.

"You promised to put the past to rest."

"Hey, I've seen your parents and accompanied you to all our old haunts. Don't act like I have my word and then sat on my ass doing nothing. "

"This is the last step. We both know it." He countered.

She bit the inside of her cheek and looked down. *How can I tell the man I'm sleeping with this is where I feel in love with his twin brother?*

"Why are you so resistant to this?"

"Why are you pushing it?" Shoving the laptop in her bag she placed the strap over her head, and turned to leave. His hand shot out and he gripped the door knob, blocking her.

"Because I don't want my brother stranded. I thought it'd be a good place for all three of us to air things out."

"And why can't we do that in your apartment?" Her gaze trained on the floor.

"Every time he's in my place he's thinking about all the things we've done to desecrate it."

"Did he say that to you?" Her chest ached. She closed her eyes against the illogical feeling that she'd cheated on Clark. *This is crazy—we were never even together.*"

"No. But trust me I know. It's in his eyes and the tone of his voice."

"Why didn't you say that?" Horror filled her. *All this time we've been slowly torturing Clark, and he never said a word!*

"I didn't have a plan to fix it then. Will you do it?"

"Go out into the woods, sit around a fire, sing camp songs, and bond with my dead bestie and my current fling? Sounds fantastic."

"Is that all we are to you?"

He pressed his body into hers, leaning down to brush her ear with his lips. "You make it sound so neatly packaged. It's not, we both know it." Wrapping his other arm around her body, he slid his hand down her waist to cup her pussy beneath the fabric of her slacks. "Right now you're wet and aching for me. I can practically smell you. Are you going to lie and tell me it could be any other man causing this response? I'm an officer. I know when someone's lying."

Unable to hold it in any longer, she whimpered and rubbed against his hand like a cat in heat. He set her ablaze like no man ever had. The connection between them took off the edge, allowed her to function and sleep. This case was personal, and sludging through the murky waters of the past hurt. When things pushed her near her breaking point on a weekly basis she turned to Carey.

Wrong maybe, but in his own way he did the same. There were no whispered words of love or talks about a relationship. Still, the nameless venture was tangible.

"I don't know. My brain is fried and my heart it bruised. What do you want from me? I'm hanging on by a thread ready to snap if any more pressure is added. This is why I stayed away from this place."

He removed his hand, stepped back, and spun her around to face him. "This is your home."

"No. Not anymore." She shook her head. This hadn't been home for a long time. A few months in town on a case wouldn't change that.

"You think it stops being that way because you don't want to deal with the past? I've got news for you, Vannah. The place you're at now is not your home. It's where you exist. You keep yourself apart from everything and everyone. Since you've been here I think I've heard you talk to Amy, your best friend, once, maybe twice."

"What do you know about my life outside of this town? We don't have deep conversations, we fuck."

"Bullshit." His jaw clenched. "It's time we lay all our cards on the table because we're not going to get another chance like this with Clark again. Why can't we make some new memories, more pleasant ones to hold onto?" Cupping her face between his large, warm hands he pressed their foreheads together. "We can send him off knowing he's loved and we'll be okay. It's the greatest gift we can give him. And for the record we do a lot more than fucking." He moved his hand down to encircle her throat. Her pulse raced and her body shook. "I haven't done more than touch you and you're ready to come. You would never give you body to someone so completely unless you cared deeply." He tightened his grip just so. "If I wanted to fuck you against this door right now, you'd let me, wouldn't you?"

"Oh God." *Yes, I would and you know it. You bastard.*

"No, he can't help you now. I should make you pay for those sharp words. Your tongue's like a switch blade it cuts so swift. But I'll wait. I have other plans for you. Now we're going to stop fighting, pack, drive to the cabin, and set things straight." Removing his hand, he stepped back and released her. Her body screamed in protest.

"Sheriff West, silent? That's one for the memory books."

"Not silent—contemplative and scheming. You might want to worry." She raked her gaze over his frame, plotting her revenge.

"I think I'd like punishment from you." He smirked. The blood in her veins began to boil. *I'll wipe that smile off your face on the drive up.*

"We'll see. I'll meet you at your place in an hour."

After opening the door, she walked out of the room with a little extra sway in her hips. *He wanted a weekend to remember... that's what I'll give him.*

"Clark." It felt stupid calling his brother like this in the middle of his bedroom. *Can he even hear me?* There was so much he didn't know about how his ghostly status worked. Clearing his throat, he glanced around. His packed bag waited on the couch. Now all he needed was his brother.

Clark appeared to his right. "You called me?" The shock lessened every time he saw him appear out of thin air. Now he barely batted an eyelash.

"Yes, Vannah and I want you to go to the cabin with us."

Clark frowned. "Why? I don't need to be the third wheel."

"This is the last step for all of us to settle things together, one last hurrah."

"She agreed to this?" Clark crossed his arms, resting his weight on the back of his heels.

"Yes. You make it sound like we're the last people you'd want to be around. I thought it was lonely where you are now."

"It is, but that I'm used to." He shrugged.

Carey sighed. "You shouldn't have to be."

"Hey, it is what it is."

"I hate that phrase, because it never makes the situation you're in the midst of any easier to swallow."

Clark laughed. "No, it doesn't. Look, don't feel like you have to throw me a bone. If you want to go off into the woods to be alone with your girlfriend it's your prerogative. I know you guys have been damn near killing yourselves to find these bastards."

"For the record she's not my girlfriend."

"What is she then?" Clark scowled.

"I don't know."

"I didn't hand her over for you to fuck this up, Carey." Venom coated every word.

"Tell me. Why did you let her go?" He wrinkled his brow and crossed his arms over his chest.

"You know as well as I do we could never amount to shit! I'm going to leave and she'll still be here. Are you purposely trying to be an asshole?"

He ignored his comment. "It wasn't worth it to stick around? Actually be there to spend what time you have left together?" He wanted to break through the hardened shell that covered him and break through to the man he saw growing more and more bitter.

"Are you trying to guilt me?"Clark clenched his jaw.

"No, I'm trying to get through that thick skull of yours!" Carey growled. "You're wasting what time you have hiding from her, and from me."

"Maybe it makes me sick to see the two of you," he whispered.

"Don't act like we make out in front of you."

"I can smell the sex on you. I see the hickeys and the tousled hair." Clark's body vibrated with anger as he grew louder with every word. "It should've been me!"

That's the admission I was waiting for ."So step up then."

"Wait—what?" Clark's voice became a blank canvas.

"You want her, show her."

"Is this some sort of game?"

96

"No, I've been doing a lot of thinking. If I want a snowball's chance at keeping her when this is over she has to make a break from you, at least romantically. I can't live with her wondering if she wishes it was you instead." *It's a hell I refuse to be trapped in.*

"And you think we'll accomplish that by doing what?" Clark asked.

"Sharing."

Clark's jaw dropped.

"Yeah I know. I'm the last guy to suggest that, but you're the other half of me, and I want this to work. Not short term, lifelong. If your ghost is hovering over us..." Carey shook his head as he trailed off. "It'll never happen."

"I don't—" Clark shook his head.

"Savannah Marie West has always belonged between us. Is it really so shocking?" Carey whispered.

"No, not really. Can you live with it?" Clark studied him. "It turns you on, doesn't it?"

"Fuck, yes it does. Once I started thinking about it I couldn't stop. Imagine it, both of us moving inside her, filling our girl up."

"Our girl... I like that." For the first time since he returned, Clark beamed.

"So, it's a yes."

"It's a hell yes."

"Thank God!" Carey tossed his hands in the air.

"Worried?"

"Yeah I was expecting you to kick my ass." Carey ran a hand through his hair and laughed.

"No, I wanted you two together. I just... I never thought it'd cut me to the quick."

"The minute I saw your face that first night, I knew how you felt. It ate me up." He shook his head.

"I'm sorry, bro. I thought I hid it better." Shame dulled Carey's excitement. "Then again, when could we ever hide anything from one another?"

"Good point… how are we going to do this?"Clark rubbed his hands together.

"Play it by ear. I'm not sure how she'll react and you know when Vannah's pissed it's best to steer clear a while. I have a question though. Can you change your clothes?" Carey queried.

"Yeah I suppose, why?"

"Might want to do that so she's not reminded…"

"Ahh gotcha. Now I'm feeling like an asshole."

"Come on. Let me show you the ropes. Give you a crash course on game." Carey walked over and slung an arm around his neck.

"Ouch. Don't mince words."

"You've been out of the loop for a while. It's understandable. Besides, I was always better with the ladies." He wiggled his eyebrows.

"And there's the ego I remember so well," Clark mumbled.

"Shut up… and follow my lead."

"Ass."

Carey chuckled at his brother's scowl. "Don't worry, bringing you into the twentieth century will be painless, I promise. You've got the whole hipster, emo thing going. We'll work with that." He patted him on his back and guided him to the closet.

Chapter Nine

Shell-shocked, Savannah sat in truck wedged between Carey and Clark in the front seat. When Carey opened the door to the apartment, revealing them both, the wind had been let out of her sail. Clark looked gorgeous in a pair of faded denim jeans that highlighted his killer ass and a soft black T-shirt, and black sneakers. Seeing Carey beside him in a similar outfit made her pussy weep.

A strange tension she didn't understand filled the cab. Clark wasn't mad. The arm he'd wrapped around her waist conveyed that. Carey drove with his hand on her upper thigh. Warm and aroused, she worried her lower lip between her teeth. They were silent. The rock music turned on low became the background.

"You're really quiet, Vannah. It's not like you." Clark brought his fingers up to twine in her hair. His cool fingers brushed her neck, and she jerked.

"Jumpy?" Carey squeezed her thigh, sliding his hand up to the area where upper thigh met pelvis. Digging his fingers in the crease, he traced up and down. Her breath stuttered.

"What are you doing?" she whispered.

"Relax, Vannah. Let us take care of you." Clark's lips brushed her ear.

Us! Her chest heaved. "I- I don't—"

"Don't think, just feel." Clark brought a hand up to cup her breast and she gasped.

"We decided it was time to get the Three Musketeers back together again for an adult reunion." Carey brushed her pussy with his knuckles, and she hissed.

"She already soaked through her jeans, Clark. I think she wants us."

Clark spread her legs wider and his hand joined his brothers. The feel of his cool fingers beside Carey's sent pleasure rocketing through her body. Her breath hitched. Her hands moved down to grip their legs.

"Are you going to let us fill you up? Take you every way possible, and make you ours?" Clark's whispered words were impossible to refuse.

"Yes."

"That's our girl." Carey circled her clit through her pants. She squirmed in her seat.

"I think she needs a little relief, Clark."

"H-here!" The chance of being seen thrilled her.

"Anywhere and everywhere." Clark unbuttoned the top of her pants and worked his way down the front of her underwear. His fingers hit her heated core like a cool breeze.

"Oh."

"You're so hot and we,t Vannah." Parting her lips, he found her stiff clit. "I used to daydream about touching you like this, watching you come apart for me." He circled faster. Her head fell back against the seat.

"Make her come on your fingers, Clark." The sensual purr of Carey's voice made her groan.

"Those sounds are music to my ear,s baby." Clark's fingers moved from her clit and sank inside.

"Clark!" She jerked, lifting her hips off the bench.

"That's it, baby. Fuck my fingers." He curled his digits, brushing a spot that made her see stars.

"Oh! God, yes!" He hit the spot over and over again. She pressed her feet against the floor, arching her back as she rode his long fingers harder. Her pussy quivered and she clamped down on his digits, screaming as she exploded. He continued to piston through her orgasm taking her higher then she'd ever flown before. A few moments later, breathing hard, she turned to watch Clark suck her flavor off his fingers.

"Mmhmm, you taste like heaven. I can't wait to eat that tight little pussy."

"First I think I need to return the favor." She opened his jeans with dexterous fingers, freeing him from his boxer briefs. Two thin veins ran on either side of his swollen length. The angry red, mushroomed tip yielded a translucent drop of moisture. She scooped up the pearl with her tongue, savoring the tangy flavor.

"Take him in your mouth, Vannah. I want to see you swallow his hot come."

Taking him into her mouth, she hollowed her cheeks and opened her throat to accept him. "Shit!" Clark buried his fingers in her hair, surging up. Using her other hand to massage his balls, she closed her eyes, basking in the intimacy stolen from a time that had never been.

He brushed the back of her throat. She gagged, opening her throat farther. Bobbing up and down she stroked his cock, twisting her hand. Her pussy flooded with fresh liquid. His grunts and moan made her core throb. As he fucked her mouth she imagined how good he'd feel inside her. Carey reached around her waist and entered her underwear. *When had the car come to a halt?* Carey fingers brushed her clit and she moaned.

"I'm going to come!" Clark let out a roar and painted her throat. Swallowing everything, she bucked against Carey's questing fingers. It wasn't long before she reached her pinnacle. Removing her mouth from Clark, she screamed. She rested her head in Clark's lap as she tried to get her breath.

"Welcome to the cabin. I had the caretaker swing by earlier and air the place out." Carey placed a kiss on her shoulder. Helped her sit up and pulled her body against him. The heat from his body seeped into hers. She relaxed against him, limp and pliant.

"Did we wear you out?" Clark asked.

"Hell, no." *I want much more than that from my boys.*

"Good, because we've both got a lot to give." Clark's voice was husky and his face a thing of beauty. Passion-glassed eyes and a large smile turned back the hands of time. He looked alive and vibrant. It was exactly the way she wanted to remember him.

"How about we take this inside?" Carey said.

"Sounds good to me. Race you." Clark disappeared, and she burst into laughter.

"Smart ass." Carey mumbled. They left the car. He paused outside the door, holding her hand. "I want you to know this isn't a one-weekend thing, Savannah."

"What do you mean? Clark won't be here indefinitely." Confused, she frowned.

"No, but we will. We'd be fools to give up what we found, regardless of how bad the timing was."

"Carey." *I did not see this coming.*

"No. It's time to stop running."

"You're right." She sighed. "If I saw you with another woman I'd want to beat both your asses. I don't know how this happened but it did and I don't want to let it go. But I can't figure out the logistics and work this case."

"I know. This weekend is about the three of us. The case isn't allowed. We'll place it on the backburner during the day. Your nights are mine now, exclusively."

The possession in his eyes branded her. *Is he serious?*

"What do you mean?" She goaded him further.

"When we get back to town you pack your things up and move in with Clark and me in my place."

102

"Yes." It was a no-brainer.

"With that settled, let's go inside before Clark pops back out here to see what's taking us so long."

He hooked her waist and led her inside the modern version of a log cabin. The pine interior was decorated with family pictures and eclectic artwork his parents had collected over the years. If the place had a theme it'd be homey hodgepodge. That's what happened when you had an artist for a mother.

"She agreed?" Clark leaned forward on the hunter green couch.

Carey nodded.

"You're ours now, Vannah. I hope you're ready."

Clark's words made Carey's dick twitch. *Ours.* They'd called Vannah *their girl* for as long as he could remember, but this was a completely different take. His brother stood from the couch.

"I've waited too long. I can't wait anymore. Bedroom now." The commanding tone made Carey smile with pride. His brother was coming into his own. He'd been cut down before his prime, but he could at least gain this back.

Beside him, Savannah purred. "Yes, Sir."

"Make yourself comfortable. We'll be there in shortly." Clark met his gaze over her shoulder.

"I like this side of you, Clark. I'll be waiting, don't take too long. I might start without you." Putting extra sway in her step, she disappeared down the hallway.

"You ready to get the bag?" Clark asked.

"Yes."

"I'll be right back."

I knew his mode of transportation would come in handy.

A quick trip to the local naughty store had gotten them everything they'd need.

Clark reappeared, black bag in his hand. "Ready, bro?"

"Oh yeah."

They walked into the room that'd always been theirs growing up. She'd pushed their twin beds together, turned down the covers, and splayed her beautiful body across the center. Stripped bare, she dipped her fingers into her glistening pussy.

"You weren't kidding about starting without us. Spread those legs wider. I want to taste you." Clark ran a hand down her thigh, gently rubbing as she complied. Moving back, he shed his clothes.

"She's addictive." Following his brother's lead, Carey stripped and moved to the side of the room to set their things on the side table. When he turned back, Clark had his face buried between her thighs. She clutched at his hair, mouth open, and eyes at half mast.

Eager to join the fun, Carey sank onto the bed beside her and slid his hand down her body to join his brother's mouth. He pinched her clit. Her body bucked.

"Oh God!"

"Are you going to come for us? Spill into his mouth so he can drink down that delicious nectar."

"Yes!"

"Fuck her with your tongue, Clark. Get her ready for our cocks."

Holding her body down with his arms, Clark complied.

"Oh, oh!" Tension stiffened her muscles. Her legs locked around Clark's hips, and she toppled over the edge. Clark slurped her down and pulled back, bringing his finger to his mouth.

His brother lifted his head and they shared an unspoken message. *Playtime is over.* Rising from the bed, Carey went to the bathroom with items he picked from up from the nightstand, and turned on the shower.

Right now Clark was taking the lead. He deserved it considering how long he waited.

They'd clean her. Get her ready to take both of them, and claim her together. He looked up a few minutes later as Clark walked in with a content Vannah in his arms.

"Are you ready to get cleaned, baby?" Carey asked.

"Mmmhmm."

Carey stepped into the shower first, and Clark placed her inside too, facing her away from him. Her warm body rested against Carey, a welcome weight he supported. He kissed her neck.

"Having fun?" Carey asked.

"Yes." The contented whisper made his heart swell. *This is going to work.*

He kneaded her breast, capturing her lips in a kiss as he made love to her mouth. Their tongues touched, gliding together in slow, rhythmic moves he felt straight down to his cock. Clark stepped inside the shower, opened the rosewater bath gel, and squirted some into his hands. Soaping down her front, Clark paid attention to the curves of her body. Her muscles jumped and Clark continued his massage. Carey wrapped an arm around her belly to keep her stable.

"That feel's amazing." She rested her head against him, surrendering herself to their care.

"I'm glad you like it. Time to rinse off." Clark stepped back, allowing the water to bead down and rinse away the suds. "Now turn around baby."

Carey helped her get into position and flicked his tongue across her lips. The playful gesture earned him a lazy smile. Her eyes fluttered open.

"You're clean baby. Time to get out," Clark whispered.

Her body tensed and uncertainty flickered in the depths of her eyes.

"Don't be nervous. We'll go slow. Has anyone ever fucked that luscious ass of yours?" Carey asked.

"N-No."

"Good. I like the thought of being your first." He slid his hand down between them and circled her entrance with his finger. "Relax baby. We're going to make it good for you." He pushed inside, savoring her gasp and the tight grip her muscles had. Meeting

Clark's gaze over his shoulder he nodded. His brother knelt down and explored her rosebud with his tongue.

"Oh!"

"No part will be left untouched tonight, Vannah. Do you like how his tongue feels?"

"Y-yes."

Her eyes grew fever bright. He continued to work her from the front, thrusting inside her slick passage as Clark readied her ass. When she began to thrust back against Clark, he knew she was prepared.

"Are you ready to feel just the tip of his finger inside you?"

"Mmhmm." She whimpered. "Ohhh." Her breathy response made him pound her pussy harder, wishing it was his dick.

"You're doing so good, baby. I'm doing to press inside you now... relax, don't tense."

Carey nipped her bottom lip. "We won't hurt you, baby, let him in, relax." He hooked his finger, and her mouth opened in a silent cry.

"Now Clark." He could feel his brother push in farther, sliding his finger halfway in and out.

"Do you feel us moving inside you, baby?" Clark asked.

"God yes, I'm so full."

They worked out a rhythm alternating in and out. Her breath came in huffy pants.

"I'm going to add another finger. Stretch out this tight little bud of yours," Clark said.

A deep guttural moan erupted. Her Pussy spasmed, locking him in a vise grip. Her body convulsed. A hot gush flowed down, dripping onto his fingers and his wrist. His cock strained against her belly. Ready to sink deep into her and find his release, he groaned.

"You ready to burn with us one more time?" Carey nibbled her ear lobe and she groaned.

"Yes."

"Let's get you out then." He nodded to Clark who stepped out first, dried himself off, and grabbed a new towel to welcome Vannah with. Patting swiftly, they stumbled down the hall. Kissing and caressing, they rekindled the flames of desire that ran rampant between them. Inside the bedroom Clark fell back onto the bed with her on his chest.

Clambering up his body, she straddled him. "I want to feel you inside me, Clark. No more teasing." She rubbed her pussy against Clark's dick, and he moaned.

"I've waited so long for this, Vannah." Clark's voice shook. "Put me where you want me."

She gripped his base and guided him home, sinking down. Connecting their lips, she rode Clark slow. Her plump ass bounced, beckoning Carey. He took the lube off the nightstand and coated his fingers. Circling her star, he spread the lube and slid in knuckle deep. She moaned. Clark's hands came up to grasp her hip, keeping their pace as Carey worked deeper inside. Dripping more of the lube down the crease of her ass, he set a gentle rhythm.

"You ready for another finger, baby?" Carey asked. "Take him in your ass. Fuck him like you're fucking me." Clark's whispered words made him grunt. She whimpered, nodding. He added a second finger, stretching her, scissoring, pulling out and pushing in.

"I can't hold on much longer," Clark warned.

"You ready to take us both inside you, baby?" Carey kissed her shoulder and placed his tip inside.

"Shit, you're even tighter here." Carey clenched his jaw. "Relax, open up." Her ass was exquisite. Tighter than anything he'd ever felt before.

"Oh!"

Clark hit a spot that made her arch, and Carey thrust home. He could feel his brother on the other side of the thin membrane that separated them.

"You're doing so good, Vannah." Carey purred. Clark pushed in and Carey pulled out, forming a rhythm. He clutched her hips, increasing his speed to counter Clark's. Sweat beaded on her skin and he bent to lick it off.

"Shit. I'm going to come!" Clark roared.

"Yes, come inside my pussy! I want you to fill me."

Her muscles quivered and Carey grunted, clutched her hair and rode her harder. Skin smacked skin. She released a guttural scream as she came. He exploded in response. Filled her with a steady stream of liquid that dripped down to coat them. His heart pounded against his chest. He placed kisses on her back, catching his breath before he eased out and collapsed beside her on to the bed. Slumped against Clark, she lifted her head to meet his gaze.

"Why the fuck didn't we do this earlier?"

Laughter erupted in the room.

"I don't know but I plan on making up for lost time." Clark captured her lips and she moaned. His cock twitched to life. *And it begins again.*

Chapter Ten

Floating on her back she enjoyed the cool water and private location. Here they didn't have to worry about anyone they knew stumbling on them and freaking out. The cool water was an amazing distraction from the ninety-degree weather. The sky was a bright blue full of plump clouds. It was as if God itself had handed them the perfect day.

It made her weary for what was to come next. The thought had no place in their weekend so she locked it away in the back of her mind. A shadow moved over her and she opened her eyes. Clark stood nearby, a mischievous expression on his face.

"Don't you—" The rest of the words were lost to the water that covered her head. She swam up, sputtering. Clark stood a few feet away, chuckling.

"Oh , you are so going to get it."

"I hope so." Desire and the sun turned his eyes into semi-precious gems. She licked her lips, unable to stay mad when her pussy ached. He moved closer and she wrapped her arms around his neck, pulling him down for a kiss. She ate at his mouth, pressing her body to his as she drank him in, hungry for every morsel she could gather. Burying her fingers in his hair, she tilted her head this way and that, wanting more connection and a better taste.

He was delicious, masculine, minty and hers. They separated for air and he squeezed her hips, bending to lick the trail of water down her neck to her chest. He slipped the triangular bikini top aside and latched onto her breast.

"Oh!" Her fingers flexed in the wet silk of his hair, pulling him even closer. The suction of his mouth had a direct line to her pussy. Throbbing with nee,d it protested the cool water that covered her to her lower waist.

He pulled away with a smack and slid his hand under her bottoms and inside her. The water added a resistance that made her eyes roll back in her head. He swirled inside her, exploring her walls with seeking fingers that hit all the right triggers. His movement created ripples in the water that rocked with her body. Rolling her hips, she rode his fingers, squeezing with her inner muscles. Her breath came in pants. He tilted her body, hit a new spot and she broke apart unexpectedly.

"Clark!" She locked her arms around him, the only thing keeping her from sinking into the water.

"You're so beautiful when you come, Vannah. Now I want you to do it again around my dick."

"Yes." Whimpering, she lifted her head, squealing when he gripped her thighs and lifted her. Her legs hooked around his lower hips, and he reached between them to move her bottoms to the side.

"I'm ready to be inside you, Vannah. It's my new favorite place." Lifting her slightly he plunged home. Setting a frenzied pace, he gripped her hips, lifting her and slamming her down over and over. The water around them churned, lapping against their skin. She tightened around his thickness.

"Shit, you're so tight, Vannah. G-Gonna make me come before I fuck you properly."

"Best part about this get away, we'll be undisturbed all weekend." Her breathless response triggered a madness in him. His eyes turned molten and he moved faster. His hips snapping against hers as he drilled inside her. A pleasurable pain hit as she stretched to accommodate the deep strokes. Digging her fingers into his shoulders she leaned back. The angle allowed them even deeper penetration.

"Oh Jesus!" Clark tensed, his cock jerked, and he exploded. His warmth spread inside her, bringing on her own miniature earthquake.

"Best time I ever had on this lake." She managed.

Clark chuckled.

"If I don't drown us first, my legs feel like jelly."

"Take your time, I like it here." She kissed his lips, coaxing him into a mind-binding lip lock. He nipped her bottom lip playfully and pulled away a few moments later.

"Hold tight."

Making his way through the water, he headed for the shore. Carey had opted to hang back at the house and sleep in, allowing them time to relearn each other. She loved his selflessness. It made her feel better about the decision to extend their love out to Clark, even if it was only for a short time. Her heart protested the thought of his departure, and she held him closer.

"I love you."

"I love you too, sweetheart." He paused to kiss her shoulder. "Are you okay?"

"Better than I've been in years."

"Same here." His breath tickled her ear and she giggled.

"Ready to go back to the cabin?"

"Sure, we've been out here for a few hours. Time to go in and get some lunch." He continued walking until they were on the shore. After fixing her bottoms he set her down, and she gathered their towels, handing him one and wrapping the other around her waist. They slipped on their flip flops, linked hands, and walked back to the cabin.

"I never imagined I'd get to do this with you, even before." Once the truth started she was unable to stop. *Confession is good for the soul, right?*

"Why not?"

"I'm not sure. I guess because we'd been best friends for so long, and you didn't show any interest in me."

"Because I didn't want to upset you or sour your relationship, How long did you know?"

"Since the summer we spent here before sophomore year."

He whistled. "I got you beat—twelfth grade."

She gasped. "No way!"

"Yes way. I've spent a good chunk of my life masturbating with your image in my head."

Her cheeks grew hot, but she loved it.

"I guess we have a lot to live up to."

"You holding my hands and looking at me with those come hither eyes fulfills my fantasies." He lifted their joined hands and kissed them.

"You're going to spoil me for all men."

"As long as that statement doesn't include Carey, we're good."

She laughed. *When was the last time I was this happy?*

"What should we do today?"

A knowing smirk lined his lips.

"Other than that."

"I thought we'd take a trip on the lake, have a picnic?"

"Like we used to?"

"Mmhmm."

"Let's go get Carey out of bed and pack a lunch." Excited, she grabbed his hand and hastened the rest of the way to the cabin. Their shoes slapped on the front porch, and she opened the front door feeling like a small child promised ice cream.

"Carey." She called out in a sing-song voice.

"Oooh that's the voice of a woman who wants something." They followed the voice to the couch where he laid watching television. Clark untangled their fingers and she sat on the edge of the couch beside Carey.

"Just a little something—canoeing and a picnic on the lake?"

He tilted his head and looked up. "That actually sounds like a lot of fun. Not that I'd tell you no."

She grinned.

Carey looked over her shoulder. "I think we already spoiled her, Clark."

"I think that's a good thing. She's quite the catch you know." Clark's teasing tone warmed her. Nothing could be wrong in the world when she was secluded here with her men.

"I'm sitting right here."

"We know, that's why this is so fun." Carey winked. She punched his arm playfully and he laughed.

"I'll go get started on lunch," Clark offered. He spun on his heel and headed to the kitchen, and Carey sat up and grabbed a fistful of hair. Pulling her to him, he devoured her mouth, claiming her with teeth and tongue. She melted into a pile of woman, pressing her chest into his. Her hand wandered down to massage his cock. He moaned and moved against her hand. Sitting up, she unbuttoned his gray cargo shorts.

"Commando?"

"Easy access."

"Hmm , I like it." Leaning over, she circled the head of his cock with her tongue. Their eyes locked and she laved him with her tongue, swallowing him as he grew to his full length. Gripping him firmly, she lowered her head and took all of him inside her mouth.

"Shit, yeah." His eyes darkened with lust, and she reached out to cup his balls.

Rolling them in in her hands, she bobbed her head up and down. His masculine grunts filled her with pride. *I'm doing that to him.* His hands twined in her hair and he thrust upward, fucking her mouth. Opening her throat, she took him deep.

"Just like that, Vannah."

She hummed and he gasped, pumping faster. His cock twitched and he let loose, filling her mouth with a wave of salty cream. When he'd given her all he had, she opened her mouth to show him the prize and swallowed it down, licking her lips.

"God, you are so fucking hot."

"Flattery will get you everywhere. I'm going to hop in the shower, change and go help Clark."

"I'm tempted to join you, but then we'd never get on the water. Come here."

She leaned in and he took her mouth, re-discovering every inch with his tongue before he pulled away.

"I like the way I taste on your lips."

Damn. "Likewise."

"Later I'll refresh your memory."

"I like the sounds of that."

She placed a gentle kiss on his lips and moved from the couch before they began round two.

He walked into the kitchen to find Clark had set out the old picnic basket and begun to make sandwiches.

"How was the lake?"

"Everything I've been dreaming off since I was seventeen."

"That good, huh?" Carey chuckled.

"Better. God, she's amazing."

"We always knew that." Carey patted his back. "Can I help you with anything?"

"Sure. Want to pack some sides while I finish up with the sandwiches?"

"I'm on it."

Before they picked up Vannah the previous night, they'd hit up an all-night grocery store and gotten the basics.

"Remember all the summers we spent here with our parents?" Clark asked.

"Yeah, I doubt they envisioned this for our future." Carey laughed. "Then again, Mom's always wanted us with Vannah."

"It's true."

Working in tandem, they relived memories until Savannah came out dressed for comfort in a pair of worn jeans and a navy blue, scooped-neck tank top and tennis shoes.

"You guys didn't have to do all the work."

"We don't mind. It's supposed to be your weekend of pampering, remember? This is us." Carey gestured between him and his brother with his fingers. "Sweeping you off your feet and making you forget about everything else."

"I must say, mission accomplished."

"We're ready to go when you are," Clark said.

"What about your swim—" He glanced over to see his brother had changed his clothes. "Never mind… starting to envy that trick."

Clark winked. "Had to get something cool with this gig." He picked the picnic basket up and held it out to her. "You carry this and we'll get the canoe."

"Deal."

She sashayed over and Carey bit his lip. *Her ass is hypnotic.* She hooked the basket onto her arm.

"Come on, the canoe's in the back."

They walked outside and he took in the beauty of the forest. Even in mid-summer it was lush and green. It'd be another month or so before the leaves begin to dim and turn in preparation of fall. One thing he loved about living in the Midwest was the changing of seasons.

The blue tarp covered the canoe set up on a rack. He pulled it away and revealed the green boat.

"Here she is."

"Still water-worthy?"

"Yeah, Dad and I took her out not too long ago on a father-son fishing trip. Come over here and grab the other end. We'll lift together."

They removed it from the rack, lifted it above their heads and turned it over, and turned to face Vannah.

"We'll follow you."

Fifteen minutes later they were paddling out onto the river. The green trees kissed the river's edge, forming a living border. A fish jumped from the water.

"I forgot how beautiful it was here." Vannah sighed and let her fingers skim over the water.

"Me too," Carey whispered, never taking his eyes off her face. She looked up and smiled.

"What?"

"Nothing, just love seeing you happy. The fishing spot should be just up a ways to the left."

"I remember," Clark said.

They steered the canoe accordingly and brought it to a stop in the inlet where they'd caught a plethora of fish.

"Ready to eat?" Vannah asked.

"Yes, I'm starving."

"I think I'll pass." Clark said, his eyes full of mirth.

"Oh my God, I am so sorry." Vannah covered her mouth.

"It's okay, you guys enjoy it."

Vannah opened the basket, took out the bottles of water and handed Carey a sandwich.

"You're corporal, but you don't have to eat?" Her words were hesitant as she turned to the side to see them both.

"Basically. I don't feel the need to do things like eat, sleep, or use the restroom."

"You don't sleep?" Carey asked.

"No, I choose to, but I could do without it."

"Wow," Vannah whispered.

"Yeah, it'd come in handy if you're working on something really important, but otherwise it makes life drag.""Yeah, I'll bet." Carey took the ham and cheese sandwich out of the plastic and took a big bite. Chewing thoughtfully, he allowed himself to simply relax. The sun shone down, warming his skin and the boat rocked in the water. It was bizarre yet perfect. The three of them were exactly where they needed to be, no matter how improbable. It had been a long time since he'd been so sure of anything.

Chapter Eleven

West!" She paused outside the door to her office.

"Yes, sir."

"In my office."

She walked inside and shut the door. "You wanted to see me, sir?"

"Take a seat."

She sank into the seat across from him.

"I want to be kept abreast of what's going on at all times. This might technically be an F.B.I. case with a federal officer. But you're in my back yard." His steely gaze commanded respect.

"I understand, Ssr."

"They want to send your partner down. What are your feelings on that?"

She pursed her lips. "I'm fine with Officer Carr. But we both know they can go over my head whenever they get good and ready."

"How much longer do you think we have until that happens?"

"Off the record, Ssr?" She angled her body.

"Of course."

She sighed. "After they hear about this new package, Dale will be flooded."

"You don't sound happy about that, West." His eyebrows rose.

"I think it could spook the murderers, and my top priority is taking them in to custody before this whole thing escalates any further."

"You think it will?"

"Possibly. It's hard to profile without more information."

"Hmm, funny thing about the mail. It's unpredictable these days. It's a shame this package was delivered a few days later then it was supposed to be."

Savannah smiled. *He's buying me time.* "Yes, sir, it's awful, the state of the postal service being what it is."

"I'm glad we understand each other. You can head out now."

She stood, grateful for the bend possible in the smaller station. The steps to her office felt like miles, and as she opened the door her hand shook. Carey looked up from his desk and nodded toward the package that set in the center of his desk.

"This one's smaller than the last." Her gaze drank in the manila envelope as she set her bag on the chair across from him.

"There was no indication of anything hazardous."

"That'd be too impersonal. They want to watch me take my last breath."

"The calmness with which you say that disturbs me."

She peered up at him and smiled. "Would you feel better if I told you I was crying on the inside?"

"No, smart ass."

"Let's go to the lab. Suit up and examine it."

"Thank God. It's been killing me staring at the thing."

"I bet." She opened her bag, dug out a pair of blue gloves, and pulled them on. Gingerly she lifted the package. The postal markings were from a small town in Texas, which told them nothing. They were clever. She'd give them that.

Ten minutes later, in blue suits and gloves, she stood side by side with Carey at an evidence table. Slicing open the top of the envelope with a scalpel, she used a pair of tongs, and pulled out a large swath of tissue held together by a brilliant red ribbon. As she undid the bow, she willed her hand to remain steady. The hairs on the back of her neck stood up.

She peeled back the layers of paper. Her heart lurched. A piece of blonde hair was revealed in the second layer. Six-inches long, the curl exuded feminine energy. Logged and placed in a plastic bag it was set to the side.

"You ready to go back in?" Carey asked once he was finished documenting, sans the date.

"Yes." She returned to unwrapping and discovered a faded wreath of purple and blue flowers woven together to make up a mock crown.

"What the hell?" Carey whispered.

"I don't know. I think these are his trophies." She waited for him to grab a plastic bag that would accommodate the new article of evidence. He returned to the table with an open bag and eased the fragile offering up, lowering it into the protective sheath.

"Then why is he sending them to you?"

"That's the question, isn't it?" He sealed the bag and she unfolded the last layer to reveal the Empress card sitting on top of a loose sheet of paper. Unlike the first one she'd received, there were no pictures cut out and pasted. At first glance the card appeared to be un-tampered with. But only a thorough examination would say for sure. Removing the paper from beneath the card, she held it up and began to read.

> Dear Agent West,
>
> I trust you enjoyed the last gift I sent. Here's another for your growing collection. I hear you're clever. So I hope you don't disappoint. Enclosed is a gift, if you're quick enough to catch it. I am ever one step closer.

"Son of a bitch is taunting us."

Carey rested his hand on her shoulder. "We'll catch him."

She nodded, unable to speak for fear he'd hear how much the simple gesture affected her. "We only have a few days with this, and then the Feds will come down and try to take over."

Carey opened his mouth and shut it.

"Yeah, I know I'm a Fed, but I work well with others. I can't say that about everyone in my department. I love my partner. Yet it's not the same as working with you. We're both close to this one."

"Do you think they'll take you off the case?"

"No, not when I'm the main point of contact. But they'll watch me like a hawk."

"Then I guess we need to get cracking. What comes next?"

"I want to compare the original card with this one. I don't see how the clue could be in the hair or the letter. Unless he uses some sort of UV ink…" she trailed off.

"Do you want me to call in forensics to go over things?"

"No. Let's hold off until we've called it in to F.B.I. There's a line I can't cross as much as I'd like to."

"Okay, let's bag everything up. Take it back our office."

"What do you think it means?" Carey asked.

The minute they'd compared the two cards they'd realized the killer's card had a series of numbers around the outer rim of the original card lacked. The Egyptian Empress sat on a throne with an Ankh in one hand and a scroll in the other. In the distance stood two golden columns covered with drawings of men from that time, and alternating blue and gold lines. Around the borders were more hieroglyphics, not numbers.

"I'm not sure. It's long, too long to be feasible as is. The question is, how does it break down? Is it in order? A jumble of numbers they threw together? It could be a victim's social security number, a birthday, the date they committed the crime. Hell, it could be a code. Maybe these numbers stand for letters."

"Or maybe these assholes are trying to get under our skin and put us even more on edge," Carey suggested.

"No, this is something. They want credit, right? To be recognized as clever, crafty, and terrifying. In order for that to happen, we need bodies and information. I'm breaking them into six or seven digit sequences, and running them through some programs to see if I get a hit. It'll take some time."

"Let's take a walk, get a cup of coffee."

"Right now?" Her incredulous expression was almost comical.

"Yeah." He nodded.

"I get the feeling this isn't a suggestion."

"No, come on." He placed a hand on the small of her back and gave her a little push.

They left their office and walked into the break room.

"Take a load off and relax. I'll make the coffee." She sat down at the break table and he moved over to the coffee station. Removing two Styrofoam cups from the sleeve, he added ample creamer and two scoops of sugar to one cup for her, and poured a black cup for himself.

"Here you are." He placed her cup in front of her and took a seat beside her.

"Thank you."

"You're welcome." Lifting the cup to his mouth, he took a sip, watching her over the rim. "You want to talk about earlier?"

"I'm frustrated as hell we haven't found anything." She growled. "They're good. Chances are there's a tie to the law, military, or a survivalist. They've kept their noses clean for far too long to not have some sort of specialized training. Their kills have to be done over at least a five to ten year span of time? It'd take time finding the right victim to match the card and plan the kidnapping out. They're meticulous and damned careful. The fact that they continue to single me out doesn't sit well. It's fucking with my head."

"You scared?"

"I'd be a fool not to be. It's clear they come and go as they please. I wouldn't be surprised if they were watching me. I'm starting to feel eyes on my back. Worst part, I don't know if they're real or imagined. They're throwing me off my game, making me doubt myself… it's a dangerous position to be in, especially now."

"Did you see someone that fit Clark's description?" He lowered his voice. "Find anything out of place at the apartment?"

"No, just a gut feeling. We're running out of time. The things they're sending are more personal, and final. They're ramping up. This last clue feels like the final straw, doesn't it? I mean, why send us coordinates?" Her brow creased, meeting in the center of her forehead. "It's like doing a victory lap before you've won the race."

"What do you want to do?" *She can't drop that on me and think I'm going to let it go.*

"Not much we can do other than watch our asses. Last night I woke up from a dead sleep. Not sure why. Maybe I heard something outside or had a bad dream I couldn't remember. I tried to go back to sleep and I couldn't until I pulled out my weapon and did a sweep of the apartment and the surrounding perimeter. Clark was off doing ghost business." *They had a don't ask, dont' tell policy with Clark's ghostly dealings.* He tamped down his anger. What the hell was she thinking venturing out alone in the dead of night?

"Given the circumstances I think that's understandable. Next time, wake me up please. What if they'd been out there and ambushed you?"

"If I didn't see them coming this time. I'd deserve it." She gritted her teeth. Her shoulders dropped and weariness was written across her face. He'd never seen her look so beaten before.

"Hey." He scanned the area outside the office. *All clear.* Leaning forward, he placed his hand under her chin.

"Are you okay?" *Is the case finally getting to her?*

"We've been at a disadvantage from the moment they contacted us. It's all mapped out and we're along for the ride. Until they drive us over the cliff we never knew was there."

"We'll get through it." He lifted her chin, forcing her to meet his gaze.

"In once piece?"

There was something more going on then she was admitting. But he wouldn't press her here—wrong time, wrong place.

"Yes. I know they have us chasing our tails right now. Eventually we'll get a break. These numbers may be just that. We'll crack it today before the end of work. Record our findings and lock it down. The Chief's stalling for us. Let's make it worth his while."

"You're right." She ran a hand down her face. "I'm just tired."

"I'm partially responsible for that. We'll have to lay off you tonight."

"Hush. Thanks for this." She waved her coffee cup at him. "It's what I needed. Now let's get back in there and get these numbers figured out."

Pushing back from the chair, she rose and he followed. Returning to their office, they settled back to work. He'd soothed her ruffled feathers. Too bad it felt like the calm before the storm.

"Holy shit! I did it! It's not *a* location. It's multiple, three to be exactin Maryland, Virginia, and Kentucky. Each located along the borders, so they could be traveled to and from easily. Son of a bitch!"

"What do you think we'll find?"

"I have no clue. Bodies, nothing, tokens from their victims." Their gazes met. "Regardless, two are out of jurisdiction. That's a lot of red tape. It'll be easier to call in the Bureau. "

"Only two?"

"One's in our back yard. We can work that one without worrying about pissing anyone off."

"Jesus." The thought of these monsters being in their back yard all this time praying on people without anyone knowing made him sick to his stomach. *How many people had they snatched from the area unnoticed?*

"Let's go talk to Chief."

Renewed by the potential break they walked to the coroner's office. He knocked.

"Come on in," the chief called.

Stepping inside, he closed the door behind him. "We cracked the numbers."

"What did you find?" Chief raised his eyebrows.

"Coordinates to three destinations, two are out of our jurisdiction, and one is just on the border." He exhaled.

"Where is it located?" Chief sat up straight in his chair.

"According to maps, a wooded area that belongs to the city," Vannah said.

"This is your case. How do you want to play it?"

"Can we take our forensics team and keep things low-key? Call for backup if we need it?" Carey asked.

Chief nodded. "Yeah. I like your approach on this one, Carr. Sound good to you, West?"

"Yes, sir."

"Start rounding up the team while I get the paperwork going. I get the feeling it's going to be a long night."

Chapter Twelve

Bone-weary Savannah stood at what had turned out to be a mass grave. The pungent stench of decomposed flesh burned her nostrils. Water trailed from her eyes, leaving salty streaks down her face. Mounds of dirt lined the clearing like giant ants had come up from the ground. Corpses in various states of decomposition were being bagged up and taking away. It looked like a zombie's burial ground. Wrapped up in plastic and doused with some sort of preserving fluid it was impossible to gauge how long some of these bodies had been here by sight alone.

"How does something like this go unnoticed?" a female member of the forensics team asked as she wiped sweat from her brow. Dressed from head to in a blue uniform that looked like scrubs, blue gloves, safety glasses, and a mask she could barely make out her pale skin and bright blue eyes.

"I think he brought them in from wherever he murdered them, because there's no way this many missing people would go unnoticed in such a small community." She ran a hand through her hair and shook her head. "I'm not sure what I was expecting. Certainly not this."

"I'm terrified of what we'll find at the other site. We pulled ten bodies out of here." Carey's exhausted tone came from her left as he rejoined her by the final body. "How long until we know what caused their deaths and get a coroner's report?"

"A couple weeks at least. This is a heavy load for our tiny facility. We'll write up all the surface things first, so at the least you'll have that."

"Thanks, Christine. I know you guys will be pulling some late nights over this. We appreciate you."

"We want to catch these psychos just as much as you do. Too close to home." Christine shuddered.

"I hear that." Carey sighed. The zip of the body bag sounded final in the hustle and bustle. Giant spot lights had been brought in as the sun began to set and the bodies continued to be discovered.

"Okay, that was our last one. We're out of here, guys," Christine gave a wave and followed the others out.

While corpses were unearthed and carried out of the woods, they'd swept the area after the investigation team and came up emptyhanded.

"Time to call it a night, West?" Carey asked. They were very careful about what they let slip in public.

She nodded her agreement. Removing the flashlight from her belt, she turned it on as they stepped out of the boundary of illumination the lights provided. Halfway from the site a stick cracked and they stopped in the tracks.

"Did you hear that?" she whispered.

"Yeah… animal maybe?" he suggested.

More twigs broke in the opposite direction.

"Turn off your flashlight." The seriousness in Carey's voice gained her corporation without question. Together they clicked off the black cylinders. The crackle and snap of debris came their way faster. Her blood roared in her ears and her throat grew dry.

Breathing in through her nose, she waited. He tugged her arm and they walked back the way they came, essentially blind except for the light of the moon. The night took a sinister turn. This couldn't be their people tromping through the woods with no lights. Keeping their pace steady, they fled. Thwack. Wood exploded from a tree, splinters and bark rained down on them.

"Fuck! They must have night vision. Run!" Two more rounds struck too close for comfort. Slivers of wood pelted her face. Spurred into action, she bolted. Disorientated she lost her bearings. *Am I moving toward the cars or back to the crime site?*

A shot whizzed from the opposite direction and they found themselves playing a dangerous game of pickle. Something hit the ground with a thug. Smoke billowed up, filling their lungs. Coughing, she held her sleeve up to her face and crouched low in an attempt to escape the onslaught.

"Son of a bitch!" Carey's voice was too far away, at least ten yards. The crunch of sticks came from her right. Straining to get her bearings, she surged forward through the smoke. *Am I closer to Carey or the killers? I can't call out until I know.*

Bending once more, she buried her fingers into the ground to center herself. She swallowed hard. Her stomach churned and her mind struggled to come up with a plan. *I cannot be captured again.*

Snap. Spooked like a horse that had seen a snake, she sprang into action and ran full-tilt. Pain exploded in her back and she was thrown forward onto the forest floor. Whimpering, she pushed up onto her knees. Locking her jaw, she ignored the pain and gained her feet to continue forward. Sticky, hot, liquid soaked the back of her shirt. Adrenaline and shock would keep her up for a bit.

She scanned the area, looking for a sign of civilization or opening in the woods. She stumbled over something hard and landed on her arm. A sickening crunch made her scream. *Dislocated.* Fear drove her. Half crawling on the ground she tried to rise once more. Heavy footfalls came up behind her and the world went black.

"Ugh." Flames licked up her back. Her chest ached. She took a shaky breath and clawed her way out of the blanket of sleep. Lifting her arms seemed like a Herculean feat, but she managed it.

A few inches and she found her movement restricted. *Of course I'm bound.* Swinging her feet, she came up short. *Bound there too, damn!* Her vision refused to clear, doubling and blurring. The dull ache in the back of her head made it unclear if she'd been drugged or simply had her bell rung. The sticky wet heat forming at her back worried her. Cool fingers touched her face, and she jerked away.

"Shh. It's Clark, Vannah. I need you to stay very still. You're bleeding pretty badly. We need to get you help."

"W-Where am I?" The floor beneath her was cool and smelled of musk. *Basement?*

"An abandoned warehouse they've set up shop in about twenty minutes out of the city."

"Did they drug me?" Woozy, she closed her eyes.

"I'm not sure." His voice shook.

"You're frightening me, Clark."

"That shot you took to the back wasn't just a bullet. It was a shotgun shell."

No wonder I'm in so much pain. "Fuck."

"Yeah."

"They're coming. Lay limp and pretend to be unconscious." Allowing her arms and legs to go lax, she closed her eyes and breathed evenly. A door creaked open. A sliver of light shone into the dark space.

"She's still out," A heavily accented voice said.

"We need to hurry. She's bleeding like a stuck pig. If she dies before we complete our ritual all of dis will be fo nothing."

"Patience, we gonna get to it soon enough."

Their Cajun accent was too obvious. It would've attention everywhere they went. They must mask it the way they did their violent, perverted, nature. These were the worst kinds of predators, wolves in sheep's clothing.

"Let's get the tools out of the truck and we'll begin."

Please hurry, Clark. Tears ran down her face. A wave of dizziness hit. Reality receded as she battled her way from the river to oblivion.

"Vannah." Clark spoke again the moment the door closed.

"Mmm here." Her words slurred.

"They're coming back. You can't be here when they arrive." The ropes were removed. Cool fingers massaged her wrists and ankles.

"I know you're hurting, but I need you to move."

"Trying." Like a car with a faulty starter she couldn't generate enough energy to move.

"Don't try, do. Now!"

Face pressed against the cool wall, she pushed off from the floor. Her body slid upward. "W-where am I going?" Breathless, only her will kept her upright.

"Stay put."

The silence that followed her indicated Clark had *popped* out.

"Here." The unmistakable slick of a safety sounded. A ridged pistol grip was shoved into her hand, and the safety clicked off. "It's your gun. Send these bastards back to hell where they belong."

"I will." *If it's the last thing I do.* Injured arm dangling at her side, she aimed at the square outlined in light. Her body swayed and her eyelids slowly dropped. The arm that held the .45 shook. The door creaked open.

Adrenaline flowed through her veins. She squeezed the trigger, emptying the rounds into the chest. The metallic scent of blood filled her nostrils and she keeled over.

Savannah opened her eyes expecting pain, but instead experienced a peace unlike any she'd ever known. A soft white light surrounded her body. Glancing down, she saw her arm was healed and her clothes weren't stained with filth and blood. The area surrounding her was lush and green. She peered around what appeared to be a park. Tree branches swayed in the wind, yielding groups of pink cherry blossom petals that fluttered down onto the grass.

"Hello?" Moving in a circle, she peered into the distance but saw nothing but land. She began to walk, cresting a hill, the field of soft-yellow daffodil, blue bonnets, heather, and red and yellow Indian paintbrushes took her breath away.

"Where is this place?" she whispered to thin air.

"The in-between."

She spun around to see Clark. "Am I dead?"

"No, but you are gravely injured. Whether you go back is up to you."

The words rocked her. "How bad off am I?"

His face twisted into a mask of despair split seconds before it smoothed over. "You've lost a lot of blood."

"If I stay do I get to remain here with you?"

"This is just a stepping stone. Heaven is so much better." He grinned. The combination of joyful and wicked made her purr.

"Do I have to decide now?"

"Yes, honey. Your body is ready to give. Flight or fight?" Leaning forward, he ran his fingers through her hair. "No matter what you choose I'm always here to support you."

The words made her choice easy.

Chapter Thirteen

An unknown number appeared on the screen of his cell phone. A million different ideas ran through his mind. Answering, he lifted his trembling hand up to his ear.

"Hello?"

"Carey, you need to get here ASAP. Vannah is fading fast. Those bastards took her down with a shotgun blast to the back and a rifle butt to the head."

"Where are you?"

"An old abandoned warehouse. The killers are dead. Right now I'm the only thing keeping her grounded, but I can't hold her to the in-between indefinitely."

"I hear you, keep talking." He jogged back inside the room.

"I need a trace on this number! Agent West managed to subdue the kidnappers, and she's hurt badly. Hang in there, West." He feigned acknowledgment as the people in the room burst into activity seemingly at once. "Just rest, conserve your energy, and stay on the line." His voice cracked. *What are we going to find when we get there?* He questioned his decision to leave once more. When he'd emerged from the woods by himself he'd contacted the station and waded back in, ignoring their request that he wait for back-up. On the scene within minutes they'd discovered a trail of blood and disturbed debris that told them she'd been taken. Immediately he'd known her best chance of survival was locating her, so he'd come back to the station to work with the techs and try to contact Clark.

"We got it!"

The rattle of information registered but his head dreamed up images of Vannah lying in a pool of her own blood. A streak of red running from the corner of her mouth. Her brown eyes, glazed and unseeing in death.

"Sergeant!"

"Yeah?" Snapped back into the present, he turned to face Officer Rodriguez.

"You here with us?"

He met her gaze and nodded. "Yeah, I'm good. Let's get out of here." Turning from the computer, he jogged for his squad car.

The twenty-minute drive was done in ten with the wail of sirens and the flash of blue and red clearing their path. When they pulled up into the empty lot the only vehicle was a white van with dark-tinted windows.

How many others have they taken in this thing who never saw the light of day again? Slamming the car into park, he stepped out.

He fell back, allowing Rodriguez to point as they approached the building. His emotions were running high, and he refused to compromise his people. Guns drawn, they entered the dilapidated stone building. Gutted on the inside, planks boarded the window, blocking the light, but large spotlights were set up to illuminate. As they traveled farther inside he spotted a hospital gurney. A silver tray lined with what appeared to be surgery grade equipment rested on a blue towel.

"Jesus Christ." His stomach churned in agreement to the comment. They point rounded the corner.

"I see blood spatter and two men down."

His muscles tensed as he waited for the signal.

"We're clear."

Two of his officers knelt beside the men, checking for a pulse.

He rushed to Savannah who lay sprawled on her back, blood pooling beneath her. *Not again, please.*

Placing his fingers on her neck, he breathed a sigh of relief. Faint and much too fast, the rhythm scared him, but it was there. The crackle of radio reached him through his emotional haze. An officer gave the okay for the medics to come in.

Bending down, he whispered in her ear. "Don't you leave me Savannah Marie! I just got you back. You said no more running, remember?"

Feet pounded over concrete.

"Sir, we'll need to look at her now."

Unable to speak he scooted back, giving the medics access. The rip of her shirt rent the air. The others moved back to allow her privacy as the medics worked.

"Carr? What's going on?" an officer asked.

He shook his head. "I'm going to get some air." Rushing out of the dank building, he let out a roar. *Is it my destiny to always be too late or make the wrong choice?* It was Clark all over again. He didn't go that night and look where it landed him. Now he took a left instead of a right, got separated, and she clung to her life by a thread.

"This isn't your fault." The sound of his brother's voice to his left didn't surprise him. "If you'd been with her you'd probably be dead."

"If you're trying to make me feel better, you're failing miserably."

"What I'm trying to do is end your pity party for one. She's in there fighting for her life. She's going to need you to keep her grounded to the Earth and later for recovery."

He narrowed his eyes. "You know something, don't you?"

"Just give her a reason to stay. You understand me?"

"How?" Clark disappeared and he found himself talking to empty air. "Okay, I'm starting to hate that."

The medics emerged with Vannah hooked up to an I.V., her body limp and unresponsive. Tilting the gurney, they loaded her into the back. *Being separated is not an option.* He turned to the officers lined up outside, dug his keys out of his pocket.

"I'm going with her. Can someone take care of my car?"

"Of course." Carlson extended his hand and Carey tossed the keys.

"Thanks. I'll keep everyone posted and call her family."

"You coming, sir?" the blonde medic asked.

"Yeah." He climbed into the back and slid out of the way as they attached Vannah to more machines. The erratic beat of her heart filled the cab.

"We're good, let's get her out of here." the burly paramedic with dark hair cropped close to his head said.

They pulled off and the paramedic began to give her shots, rattling off medical jargon to his partner in the back.

Beep Beep.

The flat line ripped his heart out of his chest and kicked him in the nuts at the same time. He gasped.

"She's flat-lining." His blond partner grabbed the paddles. Carey's vision narrowed to Vannah's face, contorted in pain as her body ceased. Bile formed and he gagged, dry heaving.

This is the woman I want to marry, form children, and grow old with. The fact sucker-punched him. He gripped his heart and forced a deep breath out from his aching chest. As the ambulance rocketed toward the nearest hospital he found himself sucked in the midst of a come-to-Jesus meeting. When life and death were on the line lies had no place.

"How is she?" The thunderous boom of Mr. West's voice pulled his head up and he rose to greet him, hand extended.

"She's stable. They're doing a transfusion and repairing the damage done from the shotgun blast."

"Who did this?"

"Off the record, the same men who accosted her and my brother." He swallowed. "She made sure they won't be harming anyone else."

Mr. West nodded and pulled his wife closer to his side.

"We're going to talk to the nurse. See if we can find out more information."

"I'm going to get a cup of coffee and stretch my legs."

Mr. West clapped a massive hand on his shoulder. A look passed between them. An understanding was formed. They both loved the woman in that operating room.

"We'll meet back up before too long."

"Yes, sir."

As he walked down the hall he couldn't help but feel lost and afraid. Being with Vannah had become second nature. Her place was at his side. Right now they should be celebrating with champagne and figuring out how they were going to make things work with their jobs. Another concern bombarded him.

What happened to Clark now? Is this the justice and closure he's been waiting for? Does he get to say goodbye, or will I never see him again? With the weight of the world threatening to crush him beneath its boot heel, he stumbled into the church chapel, entered the last pew, and hit his knees.

Head pressed against the pew, he closed his eyes.

"I know I haven't talked to you much lately, but I need you in my corner. You about killed me when you took away Clark. I was furious. I rebelled, drank, did whatever I could to take away the pain. But in the end I came back. I grew stronger and even concede, maybe I was put on this Earth to help others and being laid so low was what equipped me to do that. But this... giving me Clark back only to take him along with Vannah... that's end game. There will be no recovery or healing. I don't think I could ever forgive you. Now that's just me. We both know Vannah deserves better than to die at the hands of the bastards that stole her life once already."

"That's an interesting approach to prayer." Clark's dry tone curled the corner of his lips upward.

"It appears to have worked. You're here."

"True." Clark sat beside him.

"How long do you have?" *Please don't tell me this is our last conversation.*

"I'm not sure. Working on a new angle."

"Seriously? You might be able to stay?" His eyes widened.

"If I continue to help the two of you discover criminals."

"You agreed, right!"

"Of course I did."

He pulled his brother to him. "Jesus, that's great news! Vannah will...." His high did a dive bomb.

"She's going to be fine, Carey."

"How can you say that?" Jerking away, he scowled.

"I have it on good authority." Clark nodded.

For the first time, he exhaled.

"You know what we have to do when the time is right, don't you?" Clark asked.

"Ask her to marry us?"

Clark nodded. "We're not going to be happy with anything less."

"No." Carey shook his head. "Let's get her well first. The rest will keep."

Noise. A steady beep accompanied by a whoosh. Breathe in, breathe out. She became aware of her chest and her heavy limbs. She flexed her toes. Tensing the muscles and releasing, she worked her way up her body. The pain she waited to crash down never occurred. Fighting with her eyelids for dominance, she managed to peel them back. Her lips smacked together and her eyes adjusted to the dimly-lit room. Beside her monitors kept track of her vitals.

Hospital. A glance down at her arm revealed the I.V.

"Are you awake?" a familiar voice whispered.

"Yes." Pain formed in her throat. She cringed.

A more familiar head leaned in to her sight line.

"Clark! You're here."

"Careful, it's been a week or so since you were lucid enough to talk. Here." He held a straw to her lips and she drank, grateful for the relief.

"I wouldn't drink too much too fast. After you collapsed I called Carey and he got the others over to you. It was touch-and-go for a bit, but you made your choice and it was honored." His fingers were cool against her brow. She basked it in for a moment, resting her head against the pillows. "And you?"

"I get to stay as long as I help catch criminals."

Her eyes popped open. "Wait, you can stay?"

"They're taking an aggressive stand on the evil quota."

Tears ran down her cheek as she smiled. *I get to keep them both.* "Wait, what about the sites?"

"Mass graves in all, twenty-two bodies to match the major arcane of the tarot."

"But why?"

"Because they were more than a few screws loose."

She snickered and groaned. "A little more detail."

"Not sure. With their I.D. they uncovered their place." He wolf-whistled. "Chockfull of all things strange. Tarot cards, Runes, Crystal balls. These guys were the mayors of crazy town. I'm not sure how it all meshes together to mean something, but that's your department."

Her mind itched to delve deep into the findings.

"Yeah, you're fine I can see you're all ready thinking about work."

"Sorry."

"Mmhmm. You should hit the call button. Let them know you're awake. A lot of people have been waiting to talk to you."

"Of course."

She pressed the call button and watched as he disappeared.

"Ms. West, someone will be with you immediately."

A part of her believed she was going to die on that dirty concrete floor in a river of red. Knowing she'd taken down the Tarot Card Killers would have been enough to let her move in if it hadn't been for Carey. He was unfinished business she couldn't leave behind.

Epilogue

Y ou ready?" Carey asked.

"God, yes." She stood from the wheelchair and made her way carefully to his waiting car. While the wounds were healing nicely, one wrong movement and the pain would take her breath away. He offered his arm, helping her ease into the seat.

"Thank you." Being in this situation had taught her humility and to ask for help. Delaying her recovery by injuring herself would be pointless and stupid. Besides, it was adorable the way Carey fell all over himself trying to make sure she was comfortable.

With the death of the two they'd labeled the Tarot Card Killers something amazing happened—a shift in priorities. The driving force that compelled her to push to the brink of exhaustions had been yanked away. The demons that carved out chunks of her soul had been faced head-on and dealt with. *Nothing like a near- death experience and regular sex with my ghostly first love and his twin brother to set a woman right.*

Entering the car on the driver side, Carey started up the engine and pulled away from the parking lot.

"Is your mom still pissed you're staying with me?" He asked.

"No, she mellowed out. I think Dad must've had a conversation with her."

"I can't blame her. This whole thing scared the shit out of her."

"Me too." She reached over the console and linked their fingers, resting her head against the back of the seat.

"Where's Clark?"

"He's waiting for us at the apartment."

"You guys have something cooked up. I can tell. As long as it involves cake and just the three of us, I'm game."

He laughed. "Trust me, last thing we want to do right now is share you."

She turned on the radio on low and relaxed, happy to feel the sun on her face and the wind in her hair. *Freedom never tasted so sweet.* Dozing, she woke when the car came to a stop.

"Home sweet home."

Funny how it had become just that, a safe haven from the madness that lay outside that door. In the arms of her men she was safe, well-cared for, and understood. It was a constant ray of sunshine that cut through the darkness of her past and recent events.

Opening her door, he smiled. "Ready?"

"Mmhmm." Taking his hand, she allowed him to support her weight as she stood. "I've never been so happy you live on the first floor."

He laughed. "You'll be good as new before you know it."

"Hmph. I doubt you'll be saying that when you're ready to wring my neck."

"Luckily there's two of me. So we both get to take a turn."

"That's why we were put together. I'm more than any one man could handle."

He snorted. "That's one way to look at it."

When they reached the door to the apartment it swung open.

"Clark!" She wanted to throw herself into his arms but settled for the gentle hug.

"I missed you too, sweetheart. Welcome home." He moved back and she gasped at the scene. Rose petals littered the floor. The lights were off. Candles covered all the major surfaces, giving off a beautiful amber-colored glow.

"You guys!"

A silver bucket of sparkling cider rested on the cocktail table. No alcohol allowed with her narcotics for pain management.

"Come and sit down." Clark took one of her hands and Carey took the other. Together they guided her over to the couch where they all sat, sandwiching her in the middle, right where she liked to be.

"Everything that happened made us think long and hard about what we want," Carey whispered.

Her throat began to close. *Is this a Dear Jane Speech?* Pulse skyrocketing, she swallowed, breathing heavy.

"Do you need pain medication?" Clark's eyes were wide and full of concern.

"No, just give it to me straight. You want out? "

"What! No." Carey shook his head from side to side vigorously.

"No?" She breathed a sigh of relief.

"Jesus, Vannah," Carey held her hand between his own. "We want the exact opposite." He glanced over at his brother.

"Savannah, will you marry us?" Their voice blended together in perfect harmony, sweet and sincere. Tears formed in her eyes. *The three of them together again, forever sounded just about right to her.*

"Yes."

"I know you can only marry Carey really, but we'd consider it a three-way m—"

"Clark. Shut up and kiss me."

"Yes ma'am." He leaned in and kissed her. Carey's laughter filled her ear. Finally after all the heartache they'd found their way back to happiness, and to each other.

Author Bio

Told once 'You have to be an author, then you're craziness becomes eccentrics', Shyla Colt has always been in love with the written word and possessed a desire to write. Named after Super Girl in the comics, she often mistakes her mortality for super hero status. So, she holds many hats, Mother, Marine Wife, and writer are her top three. Writing allows her to explore new venues, face her demons, and touch others. A huge practitioner of paying it forward, and putting in what you want to get out, she hopes to inspire, enlighten, move, and entertain you with her work. Mixing humor, drama, and strong women, often with a paranormal element, she continues to soldier ahead in the writing field. One of her favorite things is talking to fans.

If you'd like to learn more or just drop a line, please check her out at www.shylacolt.com.